# Lee Changho's (Yi Chang-ho) Novel Plays and Shapes

## Volume One

### Lee Changho

Set ISBN: 1-889554-51-0
Volume ISBN: 1-889554-52-9

Editing, Diagrams, and Layout by Craig R. Hutchinson
Index by Lawrence Gross
Proof Assistance by
Anthony Blagrove, William Cobb, Robert McCallister
Translated by Sidney W.K. Yuan

We would like to thank Mr. Joohan Lee
for obtaining the publishing rights for us from the Baduk Seodang.

The earth takes *shape* like clay under a seal;
Its features stand out like those of a garment.

Job 38:14

First English Printing January 2000
Printed in America

**Yutopian Enterprises**
**2255 29th Street, Suite 3**
**Santa Monica, CA 90405 USA**
**1-800-988-6463**
**Email: sales@yutopian.com**
**Web Page: http://www.yutopian.com/go**

**1 2 3 4 5 6 7 8 9 10**

# Foreword

There is an abundance of joseki (standard sequences) in Go. The selection of the appropriate joseki however can result in a night and day difference in a game's outcome. What sets the professional players apart are the subtle differences in how they apply joseki. How accurately and efficiently one handles joseki will decide if the outcome is favorable.

By only sticking to popular joseki, it's difficult for one to get strong. However, it takes courage for one to forsake the popular joseki in pursuit of novel plays and shapes.

Regardless of the efforts one spends in analyzing a particular play or shape, the outcome of applying the novel play is often unsatisfactory due to unforeseen factors in actual games. Even if one succeeds, it still takes concerted study and analyses to perfect the play. The novel plays introduced in this book were established by a number of professional players after painstaking research efforts and analyses. The book is packed with illustrations and explanations from the point of view of amateur players, with a progressing level of difficulties.

Finally, I would like to thank Mr. Yun Chong-Su for his editorial assistance.

Song Ki-Chang

# Lee Changho's (Yi Chang-ho) Biography

(From Dictionary of Go Names by John Fairbairn)

Yi Ch'ang-ho was born 29 July 1975 in Chônju City, Chôllabuk Province, Korea. Yi Ch'ang-ho's teacher was Cho Hun-hyôn, and he started in 1984 as live in disciple, having learnt go from his grandfather at age 6.

Insei: 1984
1d: 1986 (age 10)
2d: 1987
3d: 1988
4d: 1989
5d: 1991
6d: 1992
7d: 1994
9d: 1996 (by recommendation)

Yi Ch'ang-ho won the National Youth Championship and third place in the World Youth Championships at age 9. He was the youngest Korean promoted to 9d and achieved 9d in the shortest time. He declared his ambition when 1d to be a world class player by age 20, and he achieved his first world championship title at age 17. Western name variations are Lee Chang-ho and Yi Chang-ho and Japanese variations are Ri Shōkō and Ī Chanho. He is nicknamed Stone Buddha for his taciturnity and also renowned as the foremost calculator in the end game.

# Table of Contents

**Editor's Notes:**

1.  Various conceptual models and structures are available for understanding what is happening on the Go board. Given the common usage of the terms life, death, capture, fight, etc., the conceptual model used for the basis of explanations in the text that follows is warfare. You can find an overview of the warfare model in "Go Winds" in the articles "Go An Application of the Principles of War."

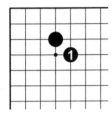

2.  When a play makes a diagonal shape such as 1, I write, "Black diagonals at 1" instead of "Black makes a diagonal play at 1."

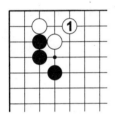

3.  When a play makes a tiger's mouth shape such as 1, I write, "Black tigers at 1" in stead of "Black makes a tiger's mouth play at 1."

# Chapter One
# A Korean Style Novel Strike

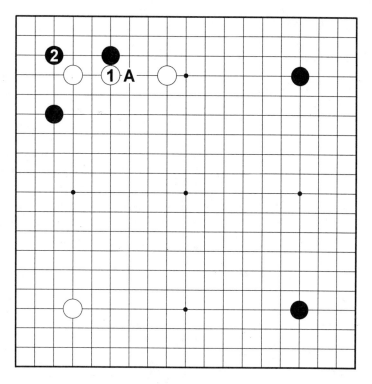

**Example 1**

This example is from the second game of seven in the fourth Kisung Tournament. In this game, Lee Changho takes black against Cho Hunhyun.

When white presses at 1, black's attack at 2 instead of a hane at **A** is a popular novel strike among Korean players. This is known as the Korean style. Generally speaking, black should definitely respond to white's press at 1. This is basic knowledge. A special characteristic of the Korean style is to break away from conventional wisdom and play according to the development of the game. Because of this, a number of novel plays and shapes have been created by the Korean players. The traditional answer to black 2 may lead to adverse effects. Let us analyze the intention of black 2 and how one should respond to it.

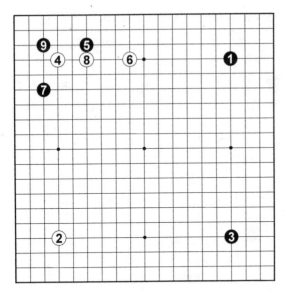

**Diagram 1**

## Diagram 1 - Actual Game

When black approaches at 5 white counters black's two consecutive star point opening with a two-space high pincer at 6. Black then approaches the upper left corner with 7. When white attaches at 8, black's invasion with 9 at the 3-3 point results in the novel strike under discussion.

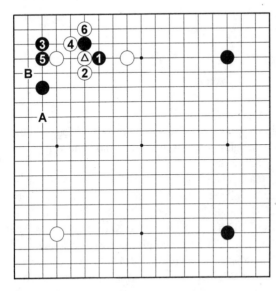

**Diagram 2**

## Diagram 2 - The Conventional Approach

After white attaches at Δ, black's conventional reply is a hane at 1. White then extends to 2, before black strikes at the 3-3 point. The sequence to white 6 is a popular basic joseki. Evaluating the outcome, one finds that white is slightly better off, because white in the future can attack at **A** aiming at **B** with sente.

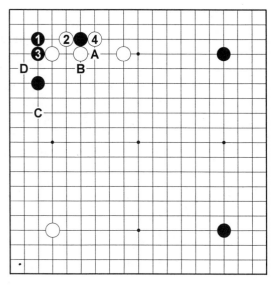

**Diagram 3**

## Diagram 3 - Black's Intention

Without the black **A** and white **B** exchange, black immediately strikes at 1 hoping that white will block at 2. Black would then extend to 3 and white's only choice is to atari a black stone with 4. This way, white's shape looks over concentrated . Moreover, a future white attack at **C** aiming **D** is not as effective.

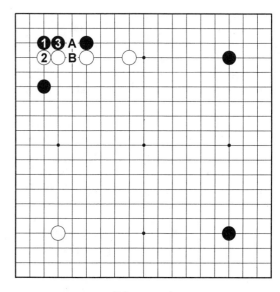

**Diagram 4**

## Diagram 4 - Blocking From The Other Side

Of course, white can also block from the other side with 2. The connection at 3 is the only defense. From here, white can choose to wedge at **A** or connect at **B**, which will lead to two entirely different outcomes.

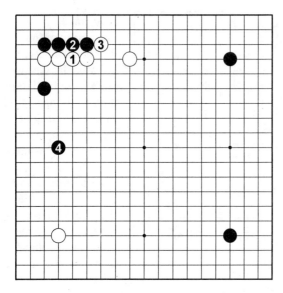

**Diagram 5 -**
**White Gets Outward**
**Influence**
White 1 is a powerful connection for getting outward influence. However, black can ignore white's hane at 3 and jump to 4. Black's fast pace is the correct strategy.

**Diagram 5**

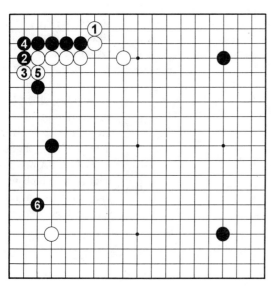

**Diagram 6 -**
**Black's Fast-Paced**
**Strategy**
Continuing, if white descends to 1, black hanes at 2 and connects at 4. After white connects at 5, black tenukies again and approaches the lower left corner. Nowadays with the emphasis on fast-paced fuseki black's approach is very attractive.

**Diagram 6**

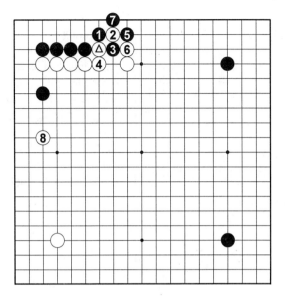

**Diagram 7**

Diagram 7 -
**Black Is Greedy**
Black's hane at 1 in reply to Δ seems to stress real territory, but is actually slack. The two step hane at white 2 is the correct tesuji. White settles the shape with the sequence through 7 before expanding his framework with the pincer at 8. White is satisfied with the result.

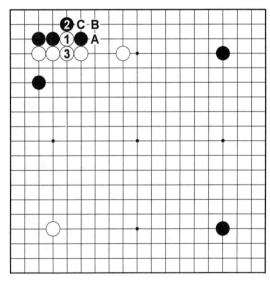

**Diagram 8**

Diagram 8 -
**An Alternative**
The wedge at 1 and connection at 3 is more complicated than simply connecting at 3. White plays this way to avoid black's fast pace shown in **Diagram 6**. Black has the choice of reinforcing at **A**, **B** or **C**.

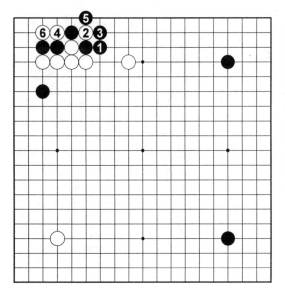

**Diagram 9 -**
**Exquisite Timing**
Extending to 1 is not favorable for black because white has the tesuji of cutting at 2. If black 3 ataris white 2, white is satisfied seizing the corner with the sequence through 6.

Diagram 9

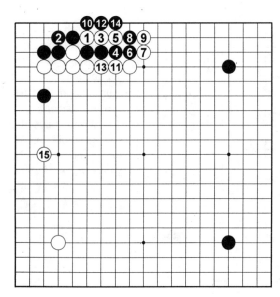

**Diagram 10 -**
**An Overwhelming**
**Outward Influence**
If black connects at 2 in reply to white's cut at 1, then white crawls along with 3 and 5 on the second line. With the sequence through 13, white uses sacrifice tactics to surround black with an overwhelming outward influence. White then pincers at 15 and is far better off than black.

Diagram 10

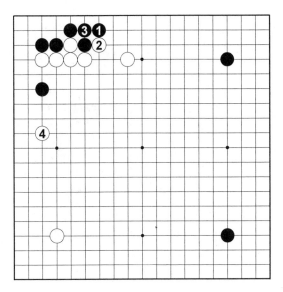

**Diagram 11**

**Diagram 11 -
White Obtains Profit
With Sente**
Black making a tiger
with at 1 allows white
to obtain profit at 2
with sente. Making
three consecutive
plays on the second
line is painful for
black, and not the
right way to start a
game. After white
pincers at 4, white
clearly has the upper
hand.

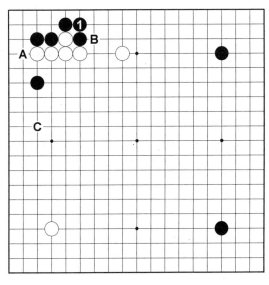

**Diagram 12**

**Diagram 12 -
A Simple Connection
Is The Only Choice**
As can be seen from
the variations above,
black's simple con-
nection at 1 is the only
choice. White can
then choose to reply at
**A**, **B** or **C**.

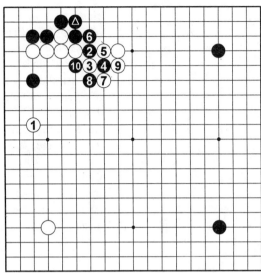

**Diagram 13 -
White Has No Follow
Up**
If white pincers at 1 in reply to △, then black hanes at 2 and 4. After black connects at 6, it is a mistake for white to atari with 7 because the ladder is favorable. Black's cut and atari at 8 is a powerful defense. White has no follow up.

**Diagram 13**

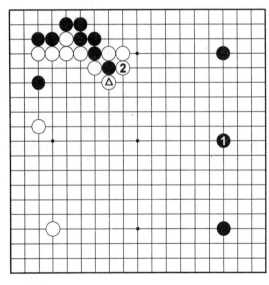

**Diagram 14 -
A Ladder Block**
If black blocks the ladder at 1 instead, then white forms a ponnuki with 2. White's influence in the center directly threatens black's three consecutive star point deployment. Black is not satisfied.

**Diagram 14**

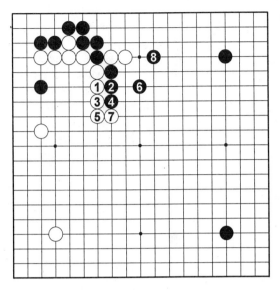

**Diagram 15**

**Diagram 15 -
An Exchange**
White's extension at 1 is a calm play. The sequence through 8 are the best replies and results in an even exchange. Black captures two white stones and secures a large territory on the top. On the other hand, white forms respectable influence in the center.

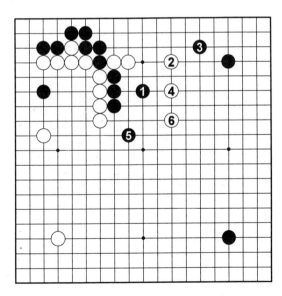

**Diagram 16**

**Diagram 16 -
A Fierce Battle**
After black jumps to 1, if white tries to rescue his two white stones, white's jump to 2 is a powerful tactic to complicate the situation. After black attacks at 3, white consecutively jumps to 4 and 6 initiating a fierce battle in the center of the board. The outcome is hard to predict.

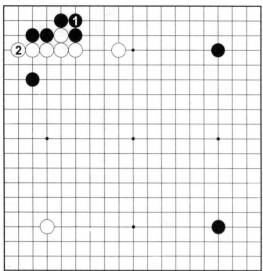

Diagram 17

### Diagram 17 - White's Tactics

Although the descent to white 2 in reply to the connection at black 1 is slow paced, it is the best tactic to secure territory. Answering recklessly will lead to adverse effects, so black must carefully consider what's the best reply.

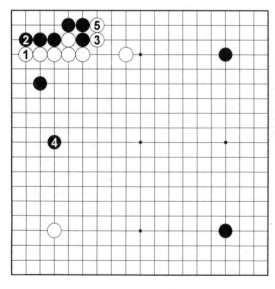

Diagram 18

### Diagram 18 - Black Is Sealed Off

The block at 2 in reply to white 1 is greedy. After white hanes at 3, black jumps to 4 to rescue the black stone on the left. However, after white seals black in the corner, black's overall position is worse.

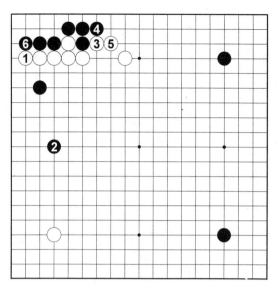

Diagram 19

**Diagram 19 -**
**Favorable For Black**
Ignoring white 1 and
directly jumping to 2
is correct. When
white tries to seal off
black with a hane at 3,
black extends to 4.
After white connects
at 5 black blocks at 6
to secure territory.
Black defending at
both ends this way is
more favorable.

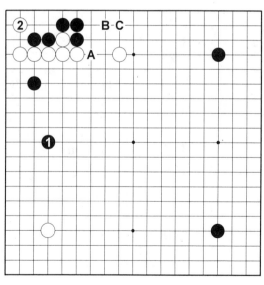

Diagram 20

**Diagram 20 -**
**White Is Courageous**
When black jumps to
1, white courageously
invades at 2-2 and
takes away black's
base. The outcome of
this exchange depends
on whether black re-
plies at **A**, **B** or C

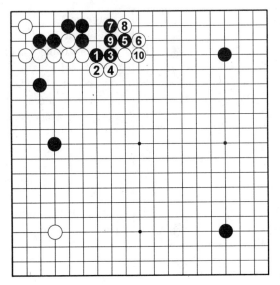

**Diagram 21**

Diagram 21 -
**Black Is Sealed Off**
If black elects to hane at 1, white blocks at 2. This result does not favor black, as he is completely sealed off after white 10.

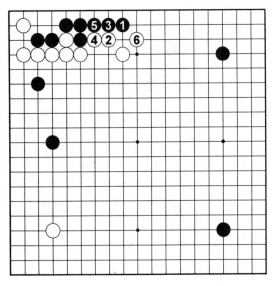

**Diagram 22**

Diagram 22 -
**Black Is Flattened**
Playing a two-space jump on the second line to settle his group is not a good tactic either. Black is flattened on the second line and is not satisfied.

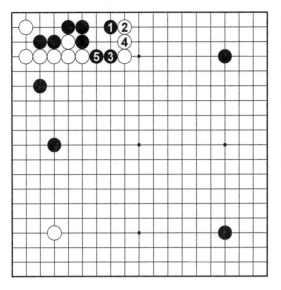

**Diagram 23**

**Diagram 23 -
White Is Reckless**
The simple jump to black 1 is black's best tactic. White's block at 2 is reckless. Black cuts white apart with 3 and 5 and develops nicely toward the center.

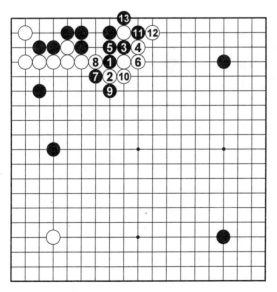

**Diagram 24**

**Diagram 24 -
A White Variation**
If white blocks at 2 instead, black wedges in at 3 to create cutting points in white's shape. Although white stubbornly resists with 4 and 6, he has weaknesses in his shape. Black settles his group through 13 and can be satisfied.

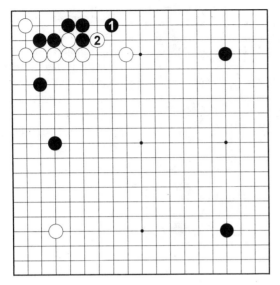

Diagram 25

## Diagram 25 - A Simple Hane Is Correct

Black's simple jump to 1 is correct in this position and the hane at white 2 in reply to black 1 is the best countermeasure.

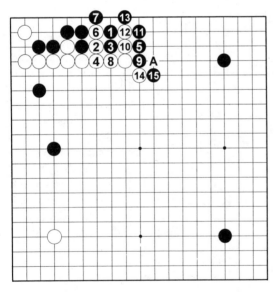

Diagram 26

## Diagram 26 - Black Forms Good Shape

After white hanes at 2, black is certain to extend to 3. When white descends to 10, black descends to 11. White ataris at 12 and black connects at 13. Black forms good shape after 15. Cutting at **A** does not work and white is worse off.

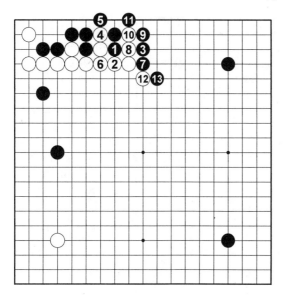

**Diagram 27**

**Diagram 27 -**
**Play Order Variation**
If white 4 in the previous diagram blocks at 2, black jumps to 3. The thrust to 4 and connection at 6 are good order. Black then blocks at 7. After black 13, the result is identical to that of **Diagram 26**; the only difference is play order.

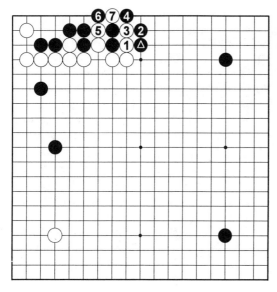

**Diagram 28**

**Diagram 28 -**
**Correct Sequence**
After black jumps to ▲ (3 in **Diagram 27**), if white thrusts at 1 instead of 5, black descends to 2. Capturing two black stones with 3, 5 and 7 is the correct approach. Comparing this with **Diagram 27**, white spent one less play and of course white is better off in this diagram.

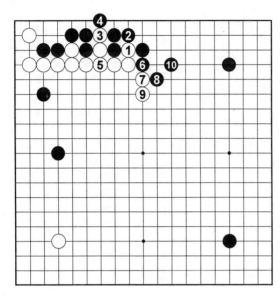

**Diagram 29**

### Diagram 29 - White Lacks Momentum

Therefore, black must block at 2 in reply to white's thrust at 1. The sequence through white 7 is inevitable. White's extension to 9 following black's hane at 8 lacks momentum. Black reinforces his link with a tiger at 10, and white missed a golden opportunity to cut black.

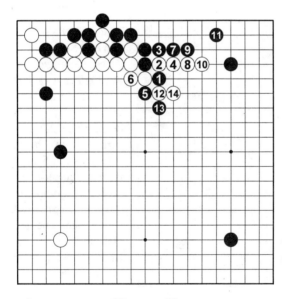

**Diagram 30**

### Diagram 30 - A Cut With Momentum

The cut at 2 in reply to black's hane at 1 takes advantage of black's weak link. Due to the presence of cutting points, the sequence to 11 is the best outcome for black. Utilizing black's cutting points, white forms a solid wall on the outside. Both sides can be satisfied with this result.

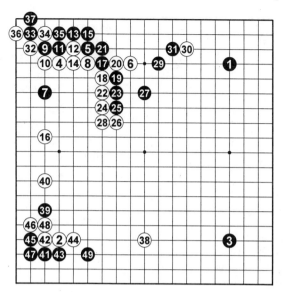

Diagram 31

**Diagram 31 -
Actual Game**
In the actual game, black 9 strikes at the 3-3 point and white blocks at 10. The local battle comes to an end after black 29, and both sides are satisfied. The game proceeded from here and black won by 6.5 points.

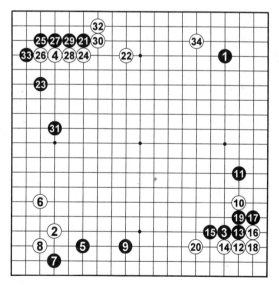

Diagram 32

**Diagram 32 -
Actual Game
Example One (1-34)**
This is the first game of the 4th Kisung Tournament. Cho Hunhyun, 9 dan took black against Lee Changho, 6 dan. When white hanes at 30 on top, black jumps at a fast pace to 31 on the left before the hane at 33. Black won this game by 2.5 points.

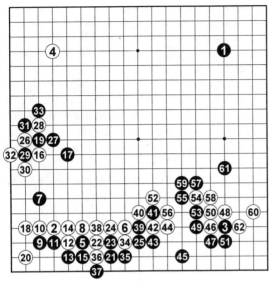

Diagram 33

**Diagram 33 -
Actual Game
Example Two (1-62)**
This is the fifth game of the 4th Kisung Tournament. Cho took black against Lee. Black taking the 3-3 point with 9 creates a chaotic battle which is difficult for both sides. White won by 8.5 points.

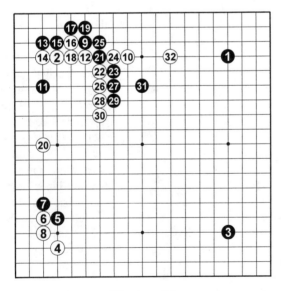

Diagram 34

**Diagram 34 -
Actual Game
Example Three
(1-32)**
This is the first game of the 27th Wangwi Tournament. Cho Hunhyun took black against Yoo Changhyok 6 dan. Following black 13, both sides proceeded in accordance with the novel play. Black won by half a point.

# Chapter Two
## A Novel Extension in an International Tournament

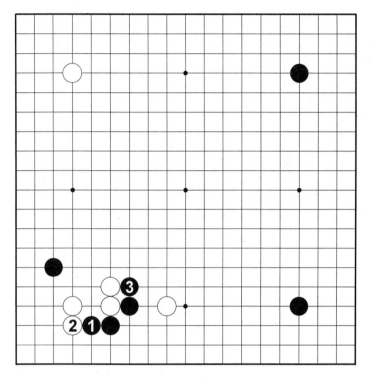

**Example 2**

This game is taken from the finals of the 6th Fujitsu International Tournament. Cho Hunhyun took white against Kobayashi Koichi. Most players in international tournaments like to play fuseki they are familiar with. Black's 3 is a novel extension used by Kobayashi, one of the top players in Japan, against the "Go King" Cho Hunhyun. Let's analyze the variations of this novel extension.

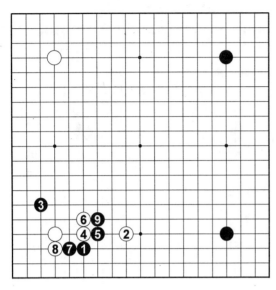

**Diagram 1**

## Diagram 1 - The Initiation Of Black's Novel Extension

In reply to black's approach to the lower left corner, white makes a two-space high pincer at 2. Black then approaches from the other side with 3. The sequence from 4 to 6 is a very common joseki. However, after 7 and 8, 9 is a novel extension towards the center that nobody had played before.

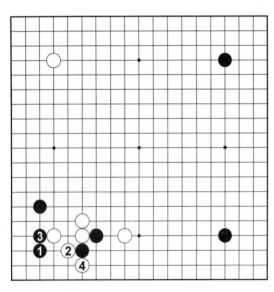

**Diagram 2**

## Diagram 2 - The Conventional Response

Black's conventional response to 6 in **Diagram 1** is to take the 3-3 point at 1. After white blocks at 2 and hanes at 4, black gets real territory with sente. However, maybe black did not like white's thick shape and aji and thus initiated this novel extension.

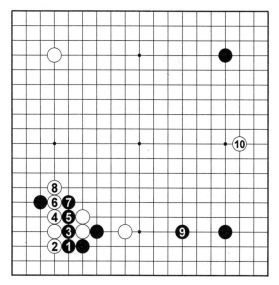

**Diagram 3 - White Gets Territory**
If black 1, white blocks at 2. If black 3, white gets solid territory with the sequence to 8. On the other hand, black's outside thickness is questionable. After black's two-space jump to 9, white splits the left side at 10, and the position favors white.

**Diagram 3**

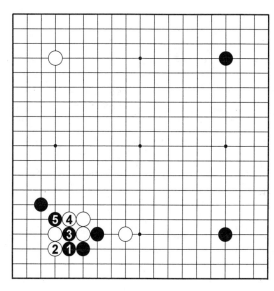

**Diagram 4 - White's Greediness**
White's block at 4 in reply to black's thrust at 3 is a mistake. After black cuts at 5, white's position will collapse. In the game of Go, it is a big mistake to risk profit in hand for uncertain larger profit.

**Diagram 4**

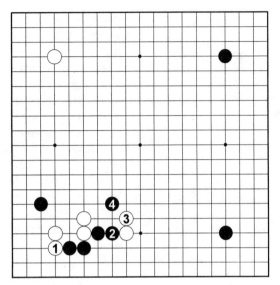

**Diagram 5**

## Diagram 5 - Black's Temptation

When white blocks at 1, if black hits at 2, white extends to 3. Black jumps toward the center at 4, tempting white to cut. A wrong play here will lead to an adverse effect for white. Therefore white must be careful.

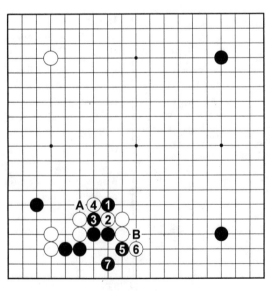

**Diagram 6**

## Diagram 6 - Black's Plan

White's thrust and cut at 2 and 4 falls into black's trap. Black is not eager to fight with white and settles his group with 5 and 7, before cutting at **A** or **B** to take the lead.

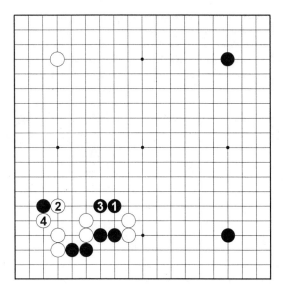

**Diagram 6**

## Diagram 7 - A Coolheaded Attachment

The attachment at white 2 on the left is coolheaded. Black is forced to connect at 3. White then tigers at 4, trapping a black stone on the left. This result favors white.

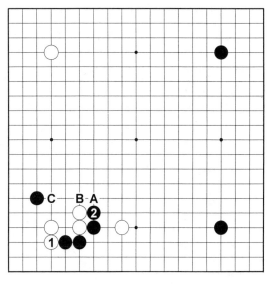

**Diagram 8**

## Diagram 8 - Choices

After white's block at 1 and black's novel extension at 2, there appear to be three choices for white either at **A**, **B**, or **C**. However, there is only one correct solution. Now, let us analyze the variations.

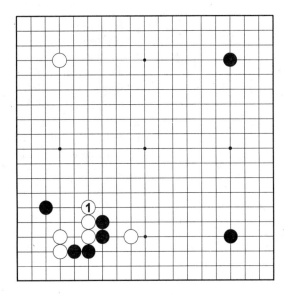

Diagram 9

## Diagram 9 -
## White Lacks
## Momentum

In a fierce battle, if one only considers one's weakness and submissively backs off, one will lose the war. White's extension to 1 seems to be threatened by black and lacks momentum.

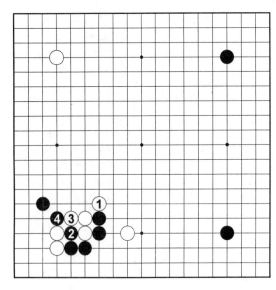

Diagram 10

## Diagram 10 -
## White Is Too Hasty

This diagram shows the variation of white's hane at 1. Making a hane at the head of the opponent's stones is an urgent point. However, white 1 is too hasty. Being cut by black 2 and 4 is intolerable for white.

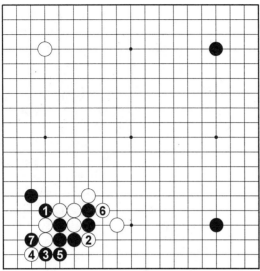

**Diagram 11**

**Diagram 11 -**
**Black's Territory Is**
**Huge**
Continuing from the previous diagram, after black cuts at 1, white cuts at 2. However, after black hanes and connects at 3 and 5, white has no choice but to capture two black stones. However, after 7, black gets a huge territory worth much more than white's outward influence.

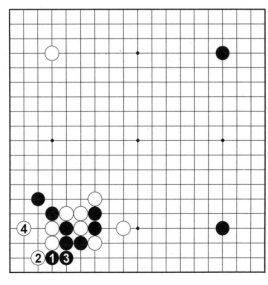

**Diagram 12**

**Diagram 12 -**
**White's Variation**
In the previous diagram, after black hanes at the urgent point at 1 and connects at 3, white plays the variation of a jump to 4 instead of capturing the two black stones. This way white stages a capturing race with black. Black must be careful here, because if he makes a mistake, white will capture black.

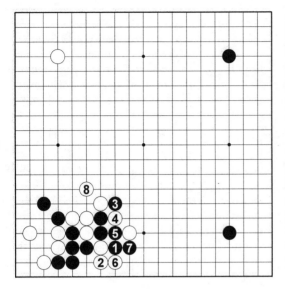

**Diagram 13**

**Diagram 13 -
Black Is Annihilated**
Continuing from **Diagram 12**, black ataris at 1 and hanes at 3, preparing to trap white with a ladder or double atari. But this is wishful thinking by black. White extends his liberties with ataris at 4 and 6 and black is completely annihilated in the sequence through 8. The game has been decided.

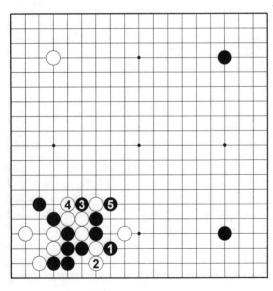

**Diagram 14**

**Diagram 14 -
Correct Play Order**
After the exchange of white 2 for black 1, the cut at black 3 is correct order. White has to extend to 4 and then black prevents the ladder with a sente atari at 5.

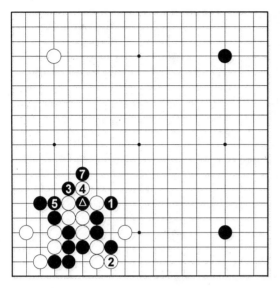

**Diagram 15 (6@▲)**

Diagram 15 -
White Is
Unreasonable
Continuing from **Diagram 14**, white turns at 2 in reply to black's atari at 1, trying to rescue his two stones. Black uses wrapping tactics from 3 to 7, and successfully traps white with a ladder.

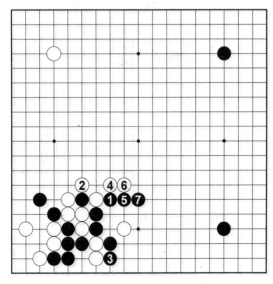

**Diagram 16**

Diagram 16 -
Black Has The
Upper Hand
White's capturing a stone with 2, in reply to black's atari at 1, is a basic defense. Black has no choice but to capture two white stones at 3. White builds a thick outward influence with 4 to 6, however, it is no match for black's large territory.

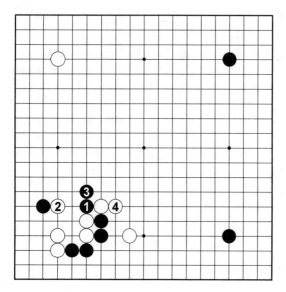

**Diagram 17**

## Diagram 17 - Black Is Unreasonable

When white hanes at the head of two black stones, if black forcefully cuts to initiate a battle then after white 2 and 4, black's position is clearly inferior. The cut is unreasonable.

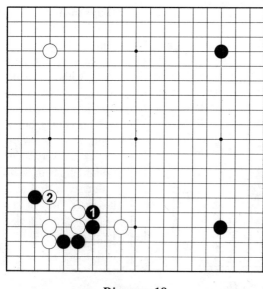

**Diagram 18**

## Diagram 18 - Correct Tactics

When black extends to 1, the attachment at white 2 is calm, cool-headed, and the only choice. If one plays flexibly according to the development of the board position, one must already be quite a good player.

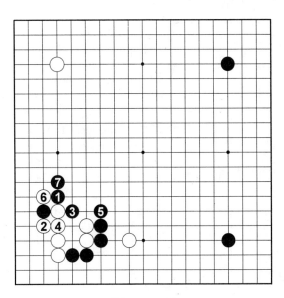

**Diagram 19 - Black's Overwhelming Outward Influence**

Continuing from **Diagram 18**, white 2 in reply to black's hane at 1 is a powerful tactic for securing territory. However, allowing black to block at 3 is painful for white. It allows black to build up overwhelming outward influence with the sequence through 7 that is not favorable for white.

**Diagram 19**

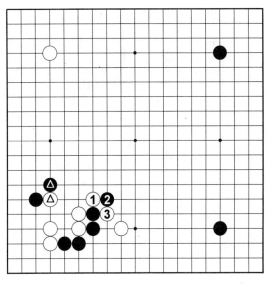

**Diagram 20 - White Forcefully Cuts**

When black hanes at ▲, white's hane at 1 works well with Δ. If black hanes at 2, white forcefully cuts at 3. This is a severe tactic which puts black in a miserable position.

**Diagram 20**

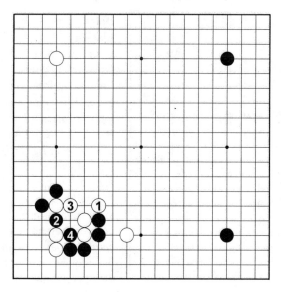

**Diagram 21**

## Diagram 21 - White Has No Follow up

White's hane at 1 before black's atari at 2 is the correct sequence. However, a connection at 3 to rescue a white stone is unreasonable for white. Black alertly cuts at 4 and white has no follow up.

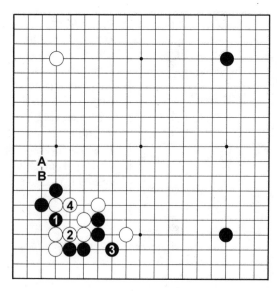

**Diagram 22**

## Diagram 22 - Best Plays For Either Side

White's connection at 2 in reply to black's atari at 1 is a basic defense. Black reinforces at 3, and white connects at 4. These are the best plays for either side. Black can now choose to defend at either **A** or **B**. Let's analyze the consequences if black jumps to **A**.

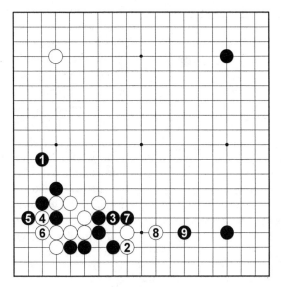

Diagram 23

### Diagram 23 -
### Black Is Better Off
Black jumps to 1 and white blocks at 2. When black escapes to 3, white hastily ataris at 4. Black forces with 5, before attacking at 7 and 9. White is worse off.

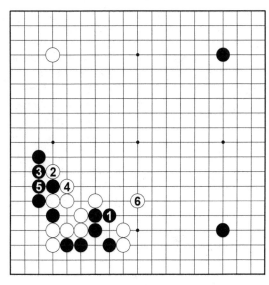

Diagram 24

### Diagram 24 -
### Black Remains In A Defensive Position
White's clamp at 2, in reply to black 1 is a probing tesuji. When black blocks at 3, white is satisfied gaining strength at 4 with sente. After black connects at 5, white jumps to 6 attacking the small black dragon and keeping black in a defensive position.

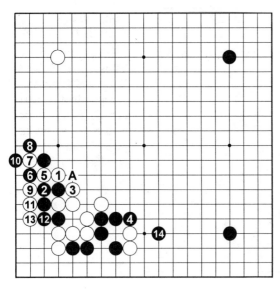

**Diagram 25**

## Diagram 25 - Black Is Favored

Therefore, black's connection at 2 in reply to white's clamp at 1 is the correct answer. White 7 in reply to black 6 is ill considered. The sequence from 8 to 14 is inevitable. Although white gets territory, black obtains profit and influence on both sides and is favored. Moreover, the weakness at **A** is a burden on white.

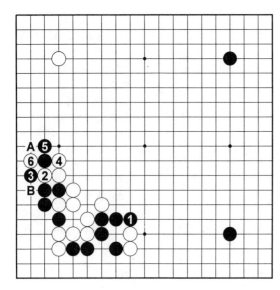

**Diagram 26**

## Diagram 26 - Correct Sequence

When black blocks at 3, white is not eager to cut, but extends to 4. This is the correct sequence. After black extends to 5, white cuts at 6. White's position is more flexible here than **Diagram 25**. After white 6, black has to answer at either **A** or **B**.

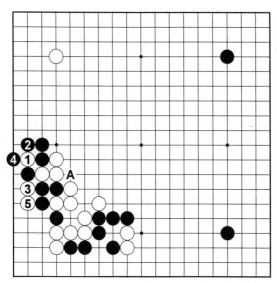

Diagram 27

**Diagram 27 -
White Has A Slight
Advantage**
If black ataris at 2, in
reply to white's cut at
1, white captures three
black stones with 3
and 5. White's stones
are more effective
than in **Diagram 25**.
Without the worry of
being cut at **A**, white
has a slight advantage
here.

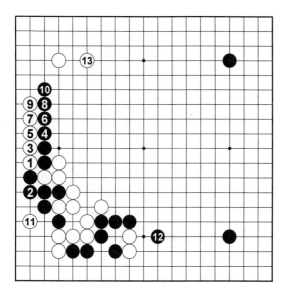

Diagram 28

**Diagram 28 -
White Has The
Advantage**
If black connects at 2
in reply to white 1,
white extends with
sente from 3 to 9, and
captures 5 black
stones with white 11.
When black attacks
two white stones at
12, white safely de-
fends the upper left
corner, erasing black's
outward influence on
the left.

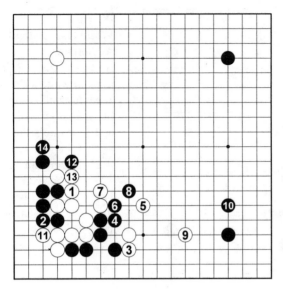

Diagram 29

### Diagram 29 -
### Best Results For
### Either Side

Black's connection at 2 in reply to white 1 is the correct approach. The sequence following white 3 is inevitable. After black 14, both sides get the best result.

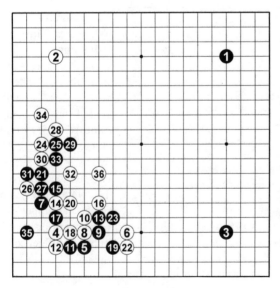

Diagram 30

### Diagram 30 -
### Actual Game

In the actual game, black made a tiger with 21. However, black 31 in reply to white's hit at 30 is questionable. The sequence of white 32 to 36 gives white the advantage. As a result, white won by 5.5 points after 265 plays.

# Chapter Three
# A Ramification of a Novel Extension

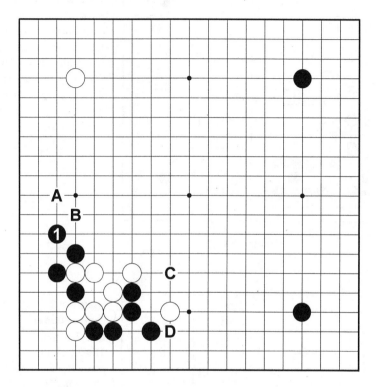

**Example 3**

This is the first game of the 1st Pae-dal Wangki Tournament (PC Communication Cup) final. Lee ChangHo took white against Cho HunHyun.

Like the development of most things in this world, if one is to reach a higher level, one must also study and research joseki in order to refine them and make them more perfect. This tiger is a ramification of the novel extension discussed in Chapter Two. After black's tiger at 1, white can choose to answer at either **A**, **B**, **C**, or **D**. Let's analyze the variations.

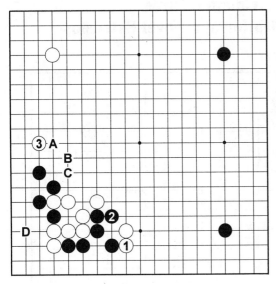

**Diagram 1**

**Diagram 1 - Continuation**
If white blocks at 1, black turns at 2. White then attacks at 3 with a powerful pincer that intensifies the situation. To this, black can reply at either **A**, **B**, **C**, or **D**.

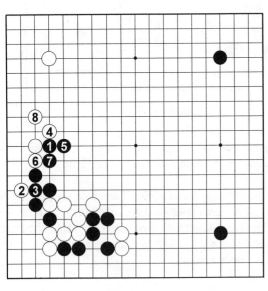

**Diagram 2**

**Diagram 2 - Conventional Development**
The attachment at 1 is probably the first reply that comes to mind. White probes with the peep at 2. The sequence 4 to 8 is the best reply for white. Black is not happy about allowing white to get thick on the left, however, black can now attack white's middle group.

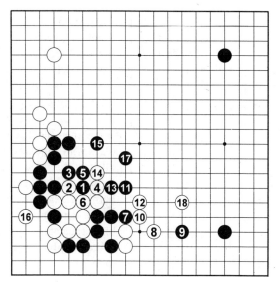

Diagram 3

## Diagram 3 - An Exchange

As a continuation of the previous diagram, black initiates the attack by peeping at 1. The sequence after white 2 is inevitable. Up to white 18, both sides make the best replies. As a result, white gains mobility with a fast pace and black forms central influence. This is an even exchange.

Diagram 4

## Diagram 4 - Wrong Order of Play

Instead of peeping at **A**, white's settling with 1 to 5 leads to a loss. The play order of black 6 and white 7 is the same as that of **Diagram 3**. Black 8 is an urgent point to establish a base. This result is not good for white. If white now peeps at **A**, black can safely block at **B**.

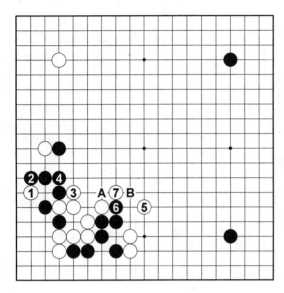

**Diagram 5 -**
**Black Is Greedy**
Black's block at 2 in reply to white's peep at 1 is too greedy. White's sente at 3 puts black in misery. White then blockades black with 5 making it difficult for black to escape. If black stubbornly extends to 6, white hanes at 7. If black then ataris at **A**, white simply extends to **B**.

**Diagram 5**

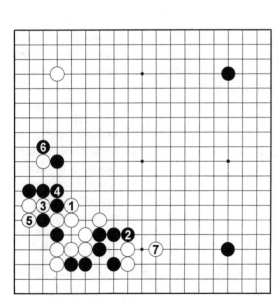

**Diagram 6 -**
**Black Is Not Satisfied**
If black tries to escape to 2 in reply to white 1, white captures a stone on the left with 3 and 5, inflicting damage on black. Black has no choice but to contain the white stone with 6. In contrast to white's fast-paced development and mobility, black is not satisfied.

**Diagram 6**

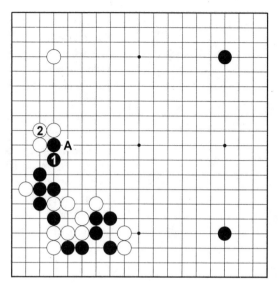

**Diagram 7**

**Diagram 7 -
Black's Shape
Suffers**
Black's shape suffers
if he draws back to 1
after white's hane in
**Diagram 4**. White 2
is another coolheaded
connection. Black of
course is not satisfied
with the outcome and
should steadfastly ex-
tend at **A** instead of at
1.

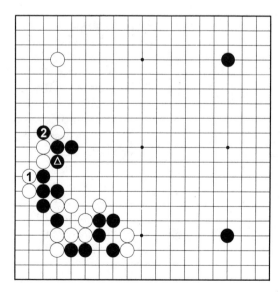

**Diagram 8**

**Diagram 8 -
White Is
Unreasonable**
Following black's
draw back at ▲, (7 in
**Diagram 2**), white's
attempt to rescue a
stone with the
connection at 1 is un-
reasonable. Black
severely attacks with a
cut at 2. The result
here will not be good
for white regardless of
how he handles the
situation.

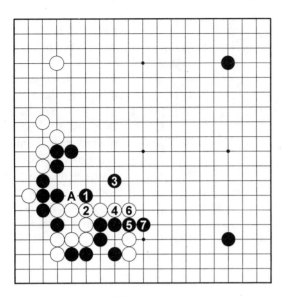

**Diagram 9**

## Diagram 9 - White Is Put On The Defensive

After **Diagram 2**, white's connection at 2 in reply to black's peep at 1 is too submissive. It is important not to make submissive plays which lead to over concentrated or heavy shapes. White is on the defensive from black 3 to 7.

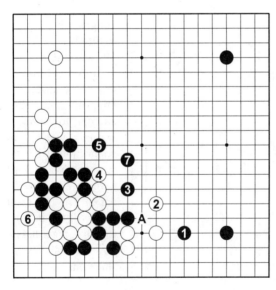

**Diagram 10**

## Diagram 10 - White's Position Lacks Influence

When black attacks at 1 (black 9 in **Diagram 3**), a tiger at **A** (10 in **Diagram 3**) is the correct response. Jumping to white 2 looks fast-paced, but it is not. It is easy to see that white's position in **Diagram 10** lacks influence when compared with **Diagram 3**.

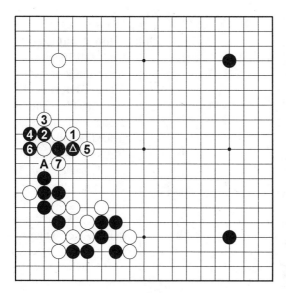

Diagram 11

## Diagram 11 - White's Variation

When black extends to ▲ (5 in **Diagram 2**), if white extends to 1 instead of **A** (6 in **Diagram 2**) seeking a playable variation, black takes control with an immediate cut at 2. White ataris at 3 with sente and hanes at the head of two black stones at 5. If black ataris at 6, the counter atari at white 7 is crucial.

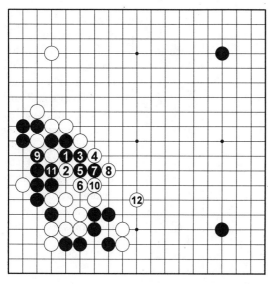

Diagram 12

## Diagram 12 - Black Is Sealed Off

Continuing from **Diagram 11**, black greedily extends to 1, and resists stubbornly with the sequence through 9. When white ataris at 10, black is forced to capture a stone with 11, and black is completely sealed off by white 12.

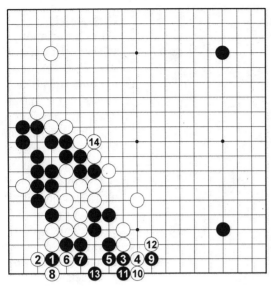

**Diagram 13**

**Diagram 13 -**
**White Completely**
**Seals Off Black**
After black is sealed off in **Diagram 12**, the black's bottom group still needs to make life with 1 to 13. Black is again completely sealed off. In the end, black's immobility greatly outweighs his territorial gain. After white reinforces his weakness at 14, white's overwhelming outward influence takes control of the entire game.

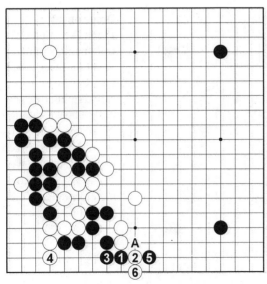

**Diagram 14**

**Diagram 14 -**
**Black Is Dead**
It is a mistake for black to hane at 1 instead of at 4. After white blocks at 2 and black connects at 3, white's powerful descent at 4 kills black. Black's attempt to rescue his group with a clamp at 5 fails because the cut at **A** does not work.

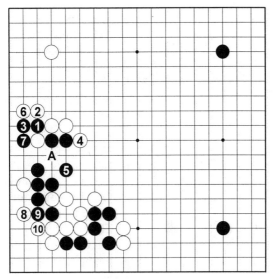

**Diagram 15 -
Both Sides Play
The Best Responses**
When white 4 hanes at
the head of two
stones, black cannot
atari at 7 because he
will suffer from
white's counter atari
at **A**. Therefore, black
chooses to reinforce at
5 instead. Both sides
play the best re-
sponses in the se-
quence to 10.

**Diagram 15**

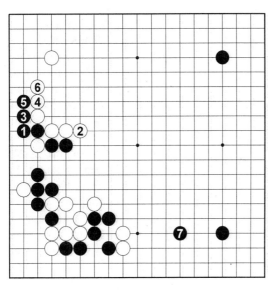

**Diagram 16 -
White's Submissive
Extension**
Afraid that black
might cut him off,
white extends to 2
instead of the hane at
the head of two
stones. This is too
submissive. Black
pushes with 3 and 5 in
sente before extending
two-spaces at 7 to at-
tack the two white
stones. This is clearly
unsatisfactory for
white.

**Diagram 16**

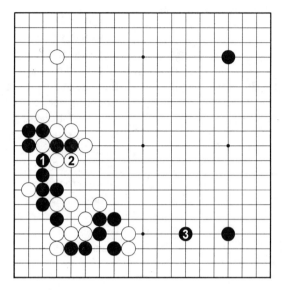

**Diagram 17**

## Diagram 17 - Black Gets Some Compensation

Under the circumstances, after **Diagram 11**, black might be reluctant to capture at 1, but this is the correct reply. Black can ignore white's atari at 2 and attack the two white stones in the bottom with 3. This way, black gains some compensation for his losses on the left.

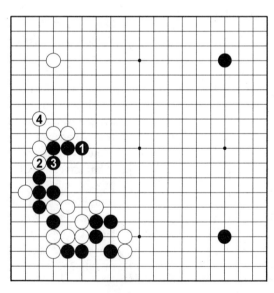

**Diagram 18**

## Diagram 18 - Black Suffers

Black loses momentum by extending to 1 instead of cutting white apart in **Diagram 11**. This outcome is almost identical to that of **Diagram 2**, except both sides have extended once more. However, missing the opportunity to cut reflects black's timidity.

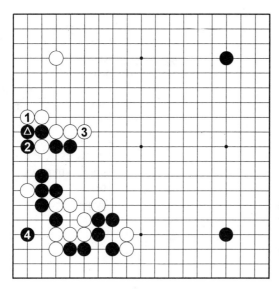

**Diagram 19**

## Diagram 19 - White Misses An Opportunity

When black extends to ▲ in **Diagram 11**, white blocks at 1 instead of a hane at the head of two stones. After black turns to 2, white must extend to 3. This situation is clearly not favorable to white. Black then jumps to 4 to take away white's base. Black has the upper hand and can attack white all over the board.

## Diagram 20 - Take Away White's Advantage

The tiger at black 1, (**C** in **Diagram 1**), tries to take away white's advantage of the peep a **A**. If white still peeps at **A**, black blocks at **B**, and white fails. Despite its strong defense, the slow pace of black 1 is its main shortcoming.

**Diagram 20**

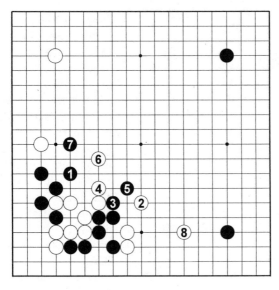

**Diagram 21**

**Diagram 21 -
Conventional
Responses**
After black tigers at 1,
white runs towards the
center with a jump at
2, threatening to con-
fine black. The se-
quence through
white's approach at 8
are conventional re-
sponses.

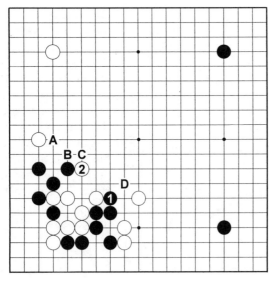

**Diagram 22**

**Diagram 22 -
White's Questionable
Attachment**
The attachment at 2
seems like an urgent
point for shape fol-
lowing black's exte-
nsion to 1. It also
looks like a probe to
decide white's tactics
for attacking the bot-
tom black dragon, de-
pending on black's
response. However,
white 2 is question-
able. Black can
choose to reply at ei-
ther **A**, **B**, **C**, or **D**.

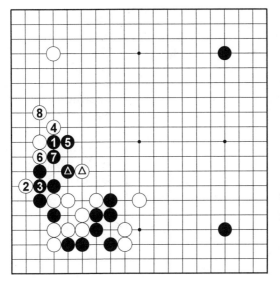

Diagram 23

**Diagram 23 -
A Bad Exchange For
White**
Following **Diagram
22**, black's attachment
at 1 is the correct re-
sponse to white's at-
tachment at Δ. White
takes advantage of the
situation by peeping at
2, and black connects
at 3. The sequence
from white 4 to 8 is
expected. The attach-
ment of Δ to ▲ is bad
for white.

Diagram 24

**Diagram 24 -
White Is Cut Apart**
What if white hanes at
1, in reply to the at-
tachment at ▲? Black
ataris at 2 first before
splitting white apart
with 4 and 6. Al-
though black loses a
stone, white has less
potential with the
three white stones on
the bottom becoming
very weak. Black is
better off.

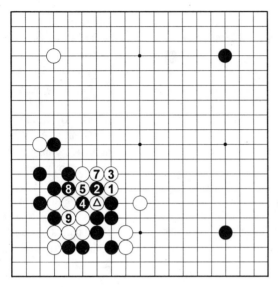

**Diagram 25 -**
**A Capturing Race**
White's drawback at 3 in reply to black's atari at 2 is the sharpest tactic for dueling it out with black. The sequence from 4 to 9 is inevitable. The resulting capturing race in the corner becomes the key to this game.

**Diagram 25 (6@Δ)**

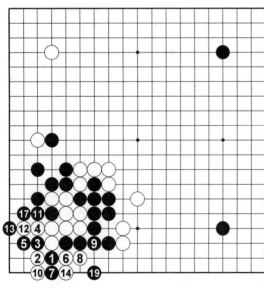

**Diagram 26 -**
**Black Claims Victory**
Following **Diagram 25**, black 1 and 3 are standard tesujis in capturing races. White resists with ataris at 4 and 6 and black descends to 7. The sequence through white 18, is the correct order. Black claims victory by jumping to 19.

**Diagram 26 (15@1, 16@7, 18@1)**

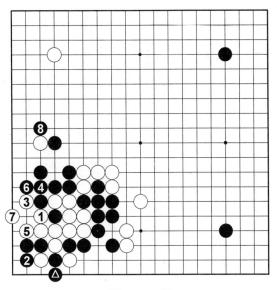

Diagram 27

**Diagram 27 -
White Makes Life
But...**
When black descends
to ▲ in **Diagram 26**,
white, seeking life,
captures at 1. Al-
though white manages
to live after 7, he is
completely sealed in
after black 8. Black
has the absolute upper
hand.

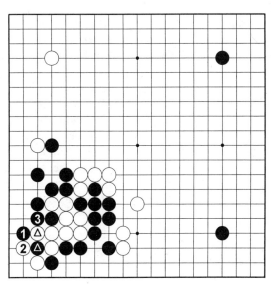

Diagram 28  (4@▲)

**Diagram 28 -
Slack Black Ataris**
Instead of extending
to 2 in reply to white's
atari at Δ, black plays
wrapping tactics with
1 and 3. These are
slack ataris. After
white connects at 4, he
can atari on either side
and capture a black
stone. This situation
is difficult for black to
handle.

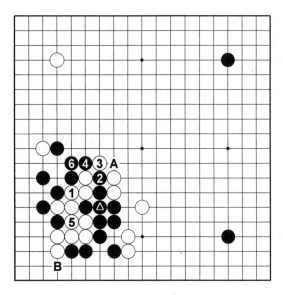

Diagram 29

## Diagram 29 -
### It's Difficult For White
What happens if white connects at 1 instead of 2 in reply to black's connection at ▲ in **Diagram 25**? Black seals off white with the sequence from 2 to 6. With the weaknesses at **A** and **B**, white's prospects are not optimistic.

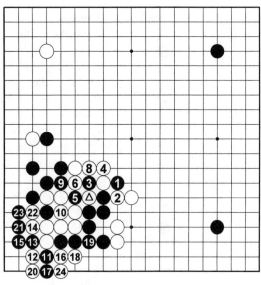

Diagram 30   (7@Δ)

## Diagram 30 -
### Black Is Dead
Black chooses the wrong order of plays if he hanes at 1 instead of 2 in **Diagram 25**. He should first atari at 3. White captures two black stones at 11 and 17 with the sequence from 2 to 24, and black dies.

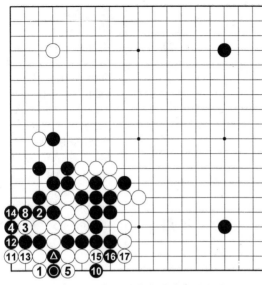

Diagram 31   (6@▲, 7@●, 9@▲)

## Diagram 31 -
## Black Is Short One Liberty

When white ataris at 1 in **Diagram 26**, black counter ataris at 2. These are common tactics used for reducing opponent's liberties in a capturing race. After white 7, it is clear that black is one liberty short and dies.

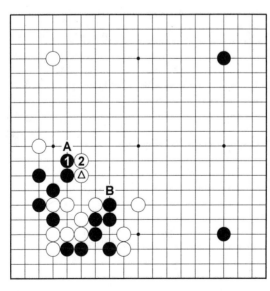

Diagram 32

## Diagram 32 -
## It's Difficult For Black

Returning to **Diagram 22**, black's extension to 1 in reply to Δ looks strong, however, it is bad. White's extension at 2 threatens to seal off the black group on the left with a hane at **A** or the black group on the bottom with a hane at **B**. White definitely has the upper hand.

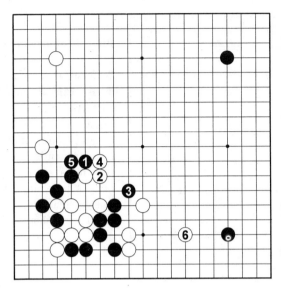

**Diagram 33**

**Diagram 33 -**
**It's Good For White**
If black hanes at 1, white is forced to draw back to 2. This indirectly helps white become thick, and leads to adverse effects for black. When black reinforces at 3 and 5, white occupies the good points at 4 and 6. The position definitely favors white.

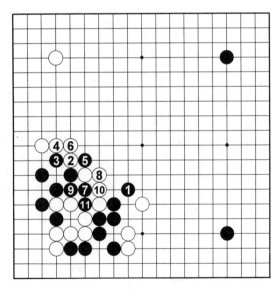

**Diagram 34**

**Diagram 34 -**
**Black's Variation**
What if black directly jumps diagonally at 1? The correct order of play is the inevitable sequence from the hane at 2 to black 11.

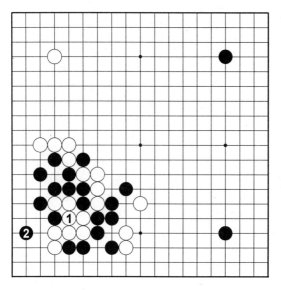

**Diagram 35 -
White Loses Big**
Continuing from the previous diagram, if white connects his two stones, then black's strong jump to 2 gains control of the corner. Regardless of what happens in the corner, white's fate is sealed.

Diagram 35

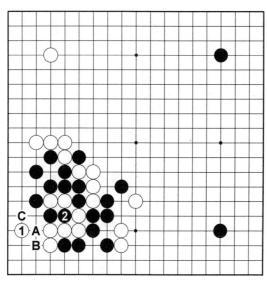

**Diagram 36 -
Tough For White To Take**
If white jumps to 1 instead, black captures two white stones, and it's still bad for white. Black can form a ko with black **A**, white **B** and black **C**. This ko is not a burden on black, but it's huge for white.

Diagram 36

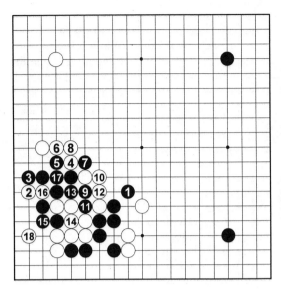

**Diagram 37**

## Diagram 37 -
## An Exquisite Peep

White's peep at 2 probing black before the hane at 4 is exquisite and the correct play order. The resulting position after 5 to 13 looks similar to Diagram 34,. But, due to the presence of white 2, black is dead after white 18.

**Diagram 38**

## Diagram 38 -
## Clear Cut Plays For White

What happens if black connects at 2 in reply to white's peep at 1? White still hanes at 3 and the sequence through black 12 is the same as the previous diagram. White makes good shape with 13 and can defend the threat of a ko by black's wedging at **A**. White is better off here than in **Diagram 36**.

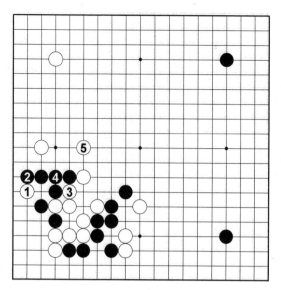

Diagram 39

**Diagram 39 -
Other Tactics**
What if white hits at 3, after the exchange of white 1 and black 2 in **Diagram 37**? Black backs off by connecting at 4 and white jumps to 5 to settle his shape. As a result, white is better off.

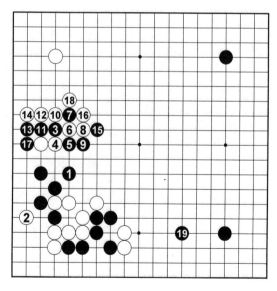

Diagram 40

**Diagram 40 -
White Is Pessimistic**
White's defense at 2 in reply to black 1 in **Diagram 26** is overly pessimistic. Black 3 is an excellent shoulder hit and in contrast, white's position is not good. Although white counter-attacks with 4 and 6, the position after black 19 favors black.

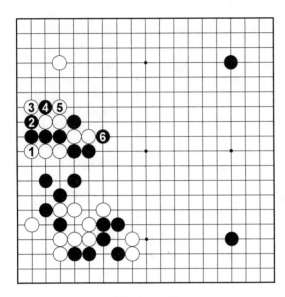

**Diagram 41**

## Diagram 41 - Ladder Favors Black

In **Diagram 40**, white 14 blocking at white 1 is a powerful attack when the ladder is favorable to white. Since the ladder favors black, white fails after black 4 and 6. White is only feeding more stones to black.

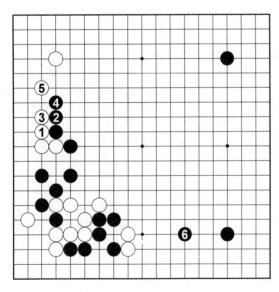

**Diagram 42**

## Diagram 42 - Good For Black

If white 6 in **Diagram 40** turns at 1, the extensions at 1, 3, and 5 do not favor white. With sente, black 6 initiates an attack on the two white stones, putting white in a defensive position. White's problem stems from his passive reply to black's tiger at 1 in **Diagram 40**.

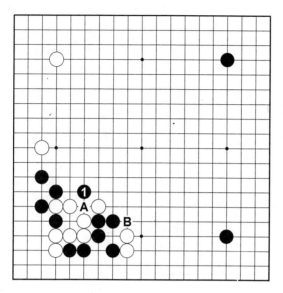

**Diagram 43 -**
**Black Probes White**
When white attacks at 3 in **Diagram 1**, black can also probe with a peep at 1, aiming to cut at **A**, before extending to **B**.

Diagram 43

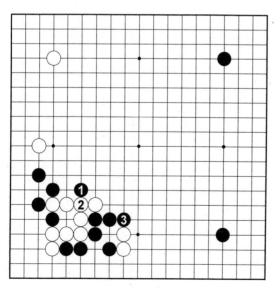

**Diagram 44 -**
**An Over Concentrated White Shape**
Almost no professional would connect at 2 in reply to black's peep at 1. The connection at 2 forms an over-concentrated shape yielding to black's wishes and allows black to easily extend to 3. Therefore, white must seek other variations.

Diagram 44

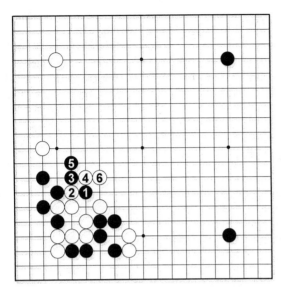

**Diagram 45**

## Diagram 45 -
## A Thrust And Cut
## With Momentum

In reply to black 1, white should thrust to 2 and cut at 4. When black extends to 5, white solidly reinforces at 6. This way, white develops his thickness and waits for an opportunity to attack the bottom black group.

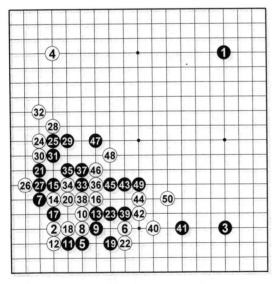

**Diagram 46**

## Diagram 46 -
## Actual Game

In the actual game, the sequence from white 26 to 32 shows the best replies for both sides. White 48 in reply to black 47 is the losing play. It should have been a defensive play in the corner. Black won after 163 plays by resignation.

# Chapter Four
# A Novel Approach That Initiated A Battle

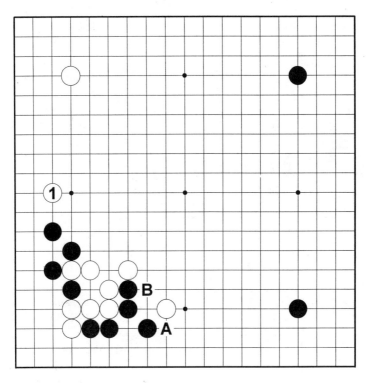

**Example 4**

This game is taken from the semi-final match of the 12th Kiwang Tournament, with Cho Hunhyun taking white against Lee Changho.

In studying handicap games, we often find examples of amateur players being greedy in trying to obtain real territory. They think that they can increase their winning percentage by strengthening the handicap stones that are already on the board. These players lack knowledge of thickness and influence. Maybe because of this, these low level players remain poor players. An even more important lesson is how to play flexibly and adjust one's strategy according to the opponent's plays. White 1 is a novel approach which initiates a battle. Without the exchange of white **A** for black **B**, how should black respond?

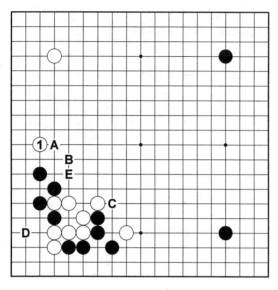

Diagram 1

## Diagram 1 -
## Black's Choices

After white attacks at 1 black has the choices of **A, B, C, D,** or **E.** We discussed possible variations of playing at **E** in **Chapter 3.** Let's discuss the options of the other four choices.

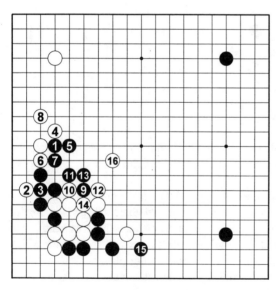

Diagram 2

## Diagram 2 -
## White Has Vitality

An attachment at 1 is the most common reply. The sequence with white's sente at 2 through 16, are the best responses for both sides. White obtains territory on the left while black obtains territory on the bottom. No one knows how the center of the board will turn out. Overall, white's shapes have more vitality than black's.

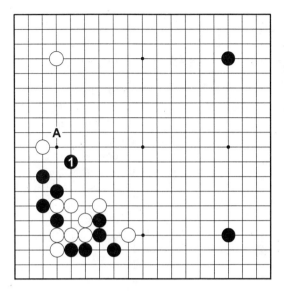

Diagram 3

## Diagram 3 - Black's Jump

Let's look at the variation where black jumps to 1. This jump aims at a shoulder hit at **A** and an attack on the bottom white group.

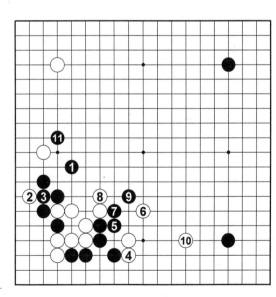

Diagram 4

## Diagram 4 - An Excellent Shoulder Hit

Black jumps to 1 and white peeps with sente at 2. From 4 to 10, white hurries to settle his shape and it results in adverse effects. With sente, black attacks with the excellent shoulder hit at 11 and is better off. Although white settles his group on the right, the life and death status of his dragon on the left is still unsettled.

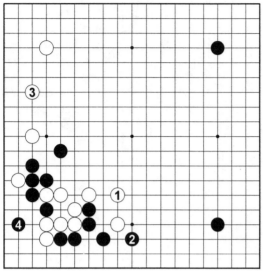

**Diagram 5**

**Diagram 5 -**
**White Miscalculates**
Instead of 4 in **Diagram 4**, white jumps to 1 and 3 with sente. This strategy is quite different. However, black jumps to 4 and destroys white's base. After black jumps to 2, black's gain in territory is obvious. On the other hand, white gets almost nothing.

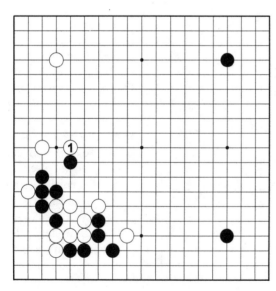

**Diagram 6**

**Diagram 6 -**
**White's Vital Point**
White must settle his group on the left before the one on the bottom. The attachment at white 1 is the best tactic. Regardless of what black does, the result will not favor black.

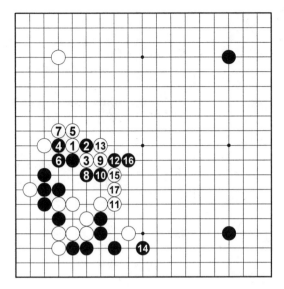

Diagram 7

## Diagram 7 - White Tesuji

If black attaches at 2, white replies with a crosscut tesuji at 3. The sequence from 4 to 17 is the best for both sides. The outcome of this exchange depends on how black handles his group on the left.

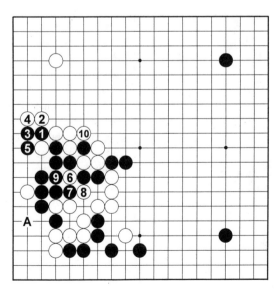

Diagram 8

## Diagram 8 - White Is Thick

Continued from the previous diagram, black cuts at 1, trying to settle his group. The sequence from 2 to 5 is the correct order of play. After capturing a stone with 10, white has overwhelming outward influence. Moreover, white can also take advantage of the sente at **A**.

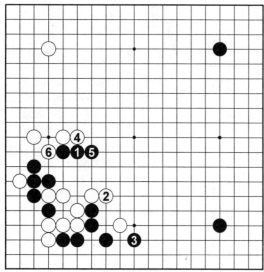

**Diagram 9**

## Diagram 9 - Black's Shape Collapses

If black extends to 1 instead of a hane at 4, white extends to 2. After black jumps to 3, white's extension to 4 does not favor black. Black extends again to 5, preventing a white hane at the head of the two black stones. When white tigers at 6, black's shape collapses.

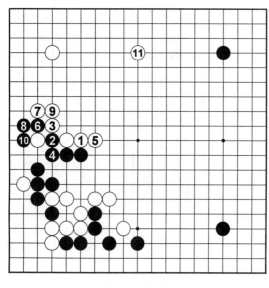

**Diagram 10**

## Diagram 10 - Black's Variation

A wedge at 2 might be the best choice for black. White reinforces his shape with the sequence from 3 to 10, before taking the vital point at 11. White's shape has vitality.

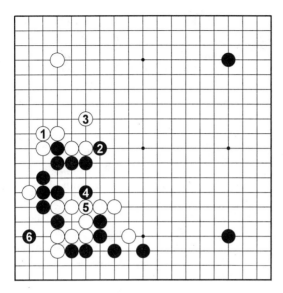

**Diagram 11**

### Diagram 11 - White is Greedy For Territory

White's connection at 1 shows his greediness for territory. Black's hane at 2 at the head of two white stones is severe. After the exchange of black 4 for white 5, black jumps to 6. The entire white group is baseless. The difference is huge when compared to **Diagram 10**.

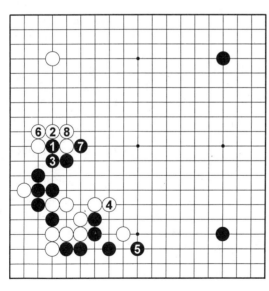

**Diagram 12**

### Diagram 12 - A Useless Wedge

What if black wedges in right away at 1? White's outside atari at 2 is the correct response. After the exchange of white 4 for black 5, white connects at 6 and forms good shape nullifying the effectiveness of the wedge at black 1.

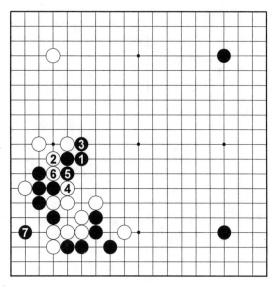

**Diagram 13**

**Diagram 13 -**
**White Misses The**
**Urgent Point**

A white tiger at 2 in reply to the extension at black 1 is too conservative. White misses the mutual urgent point of black 3. White can cut black apart with the sequence from 4 to 6. However, after jumping to 7, black is no longer under attack. White has miscalculated.

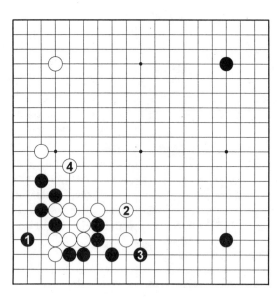

**Diagram 14**

**Diagram 14 -**
**Black Is Sealed Off**

Although black 1 is an urgent point for establishing a base, white can seal black in with 2 and 4 and the position is bad for black. Although the result is difficult to predict, one can conclude that black 1 is not a good jump.

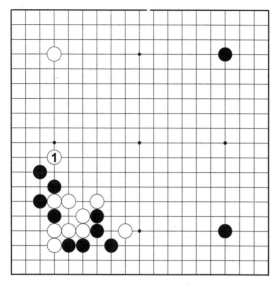

Diagram 15

## Diagram 15 - White's Intention

In contrast with **Example 4**, white 1 is a common approach in actual games, intending to leisurely take care of the left side before attacking the black group in the bottom.

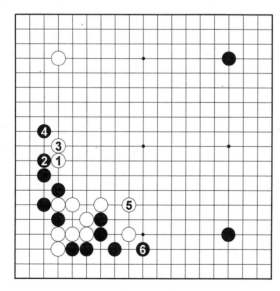

Diagram 16

## Diagram 16 - White Miscalculates

The sequence of 1 to 4 is the correct play order. White's jump to 5 is slack, putting too much emphases on safety. After jumping to 6, black successfully settles his groups on both sides. White has miscalculated.

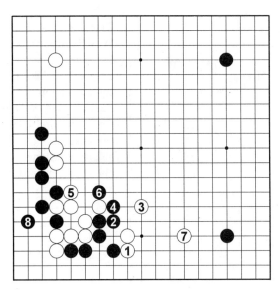

Diagram 17

### Diagram 17 - White's Momentum

White blocks at 1 (instead of jumping to 5 in the previous diagram) and tries to fully utilize his outward influence as a counter to black's territory on the left. White then attacks black with the sequence through 7. After black jumps to 8, the end result is difficult to predict.

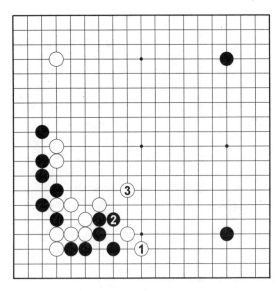

Diagram 18

### Diagram 18 - White's Trap

Instead of blocking as in the previous diagram, white diagonals at 1, trying to trick black. After black turns at 2, white jumps to 3. Black has to be careful or he will fall into white's trap.

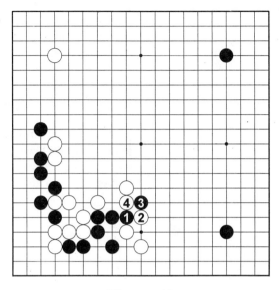

**Diagram 19**

**Diagram 19 -**
**White Succeeds**
Continuing from the previous diagram, if black simply thrusts to 1, he falls into white's trap. If black hanes at 3, intending to start a capturing race with white, then white's cut at 4 puts black in an unfavorable position of having to make life. White's trap succeeds.

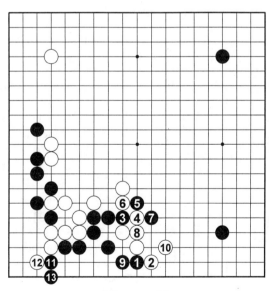

**Diagram 20**

**Diagram 20 -**
**Correct Response**
Black should attach at 1 instead. After white blocks at 2, black crosscuts with 3 and 5 in correct order. White settles his shape with the sequence through 10. Black, on the other hand, makes life with 11 and 13, before attacking the white group on the bottom. This is a result of black recognizing white's trick play.

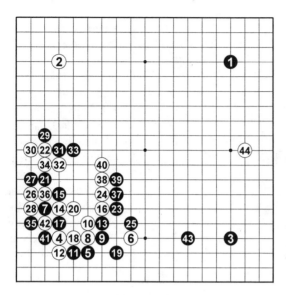

**Diagram 21**

### Diagram 21 - Actual Game

In the actual game, an exchange resulted with the sequence from 13 to 42. White gets territory and black gets outward influence. White won the game by resignation after 164 plays.

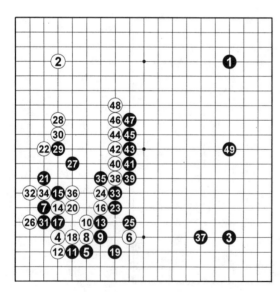

**Diagram 22**

### Diagram 22 - Another Example

This example is taken from the 3rd game of a five game match in the 11th Daewang Tournament. Lee was 6 dan at that time, taking black against Cho Hunhyun 9 dan. White obtains tremendous territory on the left. On the other hand, black gets magnificent outward influence. White won by resignation after 124 plays.

# Chapter Five
## A Novel Attachment Based on Detailed Planning

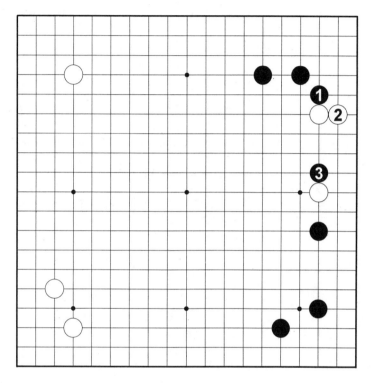

**Example 5**

This example is from the first game of a five game match, in the 37$^{th}$ Guksu Tournament. Lee took black against Cho Hunhyun.

In this game, Lee played an exquisite novel attachment which led Cho to miscalculate and lose the game. Lee then took the 2$^{nd}$ and 3$^{rd}$ games to capture the Guksu crown. By winning other titles including Kisung, Lee had 10 major titles under his belt and became the undisputed top player on the Korean Go scene. Let us analyze this novel attachment.

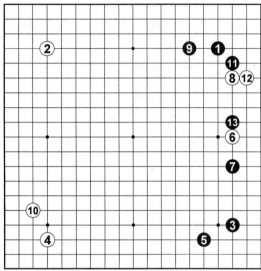

**Diagram 1**

## Diagram 1 - Actual Game

Black opens the game solidly with 1, 3 and 5. The game proceeds smoothly from the split at 6 to the one space jump to 9. White's corner closure at 10 is a fast-paced strategy used by Cho. When black diagonals at 11, white descends to 12. Black's novel attachment at 13 is the starting point of our discussion.

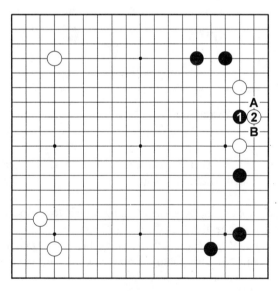

**Diagram 2**

## Diagram 2 - Conventional Train Of Thought

Black's invasion at 1 is the most common attack which comes to mind. White tries to connect with the common attachment at 2. Black can then hane at **A** or **B**.

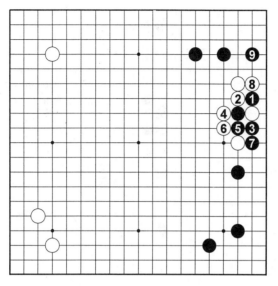

**Diagram 3**

**Diagram 3 - Black Successfully Settles Both Groups**
If black hanes at 1, white will absolutely cut at 2. After black ataris at 3, white counter ataris at 4. The sequence through white 8 is common knowledge. Black defends his corner group at 9 and successfully settles both groups. This does not favor white.

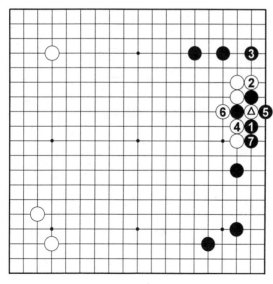

**Diagram 4  (8@Δ)**

**Diagram 4 - Black Lacks Ko Threats**
When black ataris at 1, a counter atari at white 2 is strong. If black wants to reproduce the result of **Diagram 3** and jumps to 3, white ataris with a tesuji at 4. The sequence from 5 to the initiation of a ko by white at 8 is inevitable. White is favored due to a lack of ko threats in the beginning of a game.

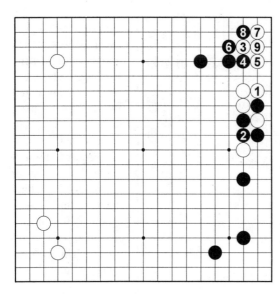

**Diagram 5**

## Diagram 5 - Basic Joseki

Black's connection at 2 in reply to white's atari at 1 is the correct response. After white invades at 3-3 the sequence from 4 to 10 shows the best responses from both sides. As a result, black successfully settles his two groups. But white also easily stabilizes his group.

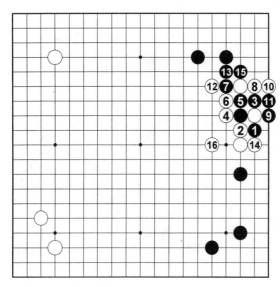

**Diagram 6**

## Diagram 6 - Black's Territory Is Big

If black hanes on the other side at 1 (B in **Diagram 2**), white can sacrifice his stones with the sequence through 16, getting fair sized outward influence. However, white loses sente and black's large territory makes it uncomfortable for white.

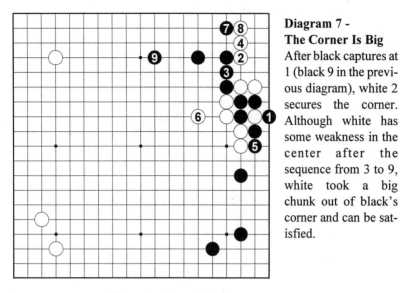

Diagram 7

### Diagram 7 - The Corner Is Big

After black captures at 1 (black 9 in the previous diagram), white 2 secures the corner. Although white has some weakness in the center after the sequence from 3 to 9, white took a big chunk out of black's corner and can be satisfied.

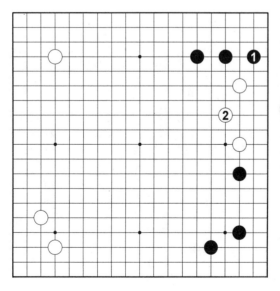

Diagram 8

### Diagram 8 - It's Unappealing For Black

Not wanting to lose the corner, black defends at 1, instead of invading white's three-space extension. However allowing white to reinforce at 2 is still not favorable for black.

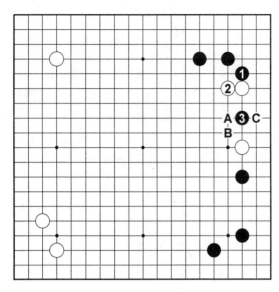

**Diagram 9**

### Diagram 9 - Black Is Successful

Black's hit at 1 warrants white's extension at 2. Without the possibility of an invasion at 3, black 1 is not recommended, because it strengthens white. After black invades at 3, white can elect to defend at **A**, **B** or **C**.

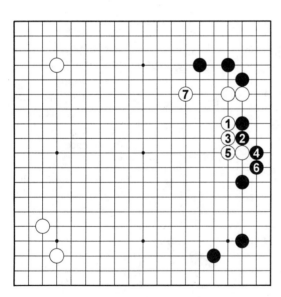

**Diagram 10**

### Diagram 10 - White Is Thick

When white attaches at 1, black tries to connect with the sequence from 2 to 6. However, white is thick after a jump to 7. Therefore, black should try other tactics to prevent white from easily settling his group.

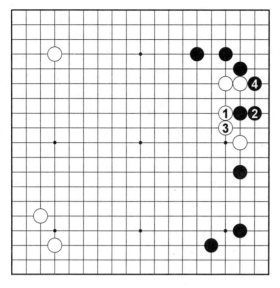

**Diagram 11 -
Black Is Favored**
Black descends to 2
aiming to connect to
either side. After
white reinforces at 3,
black connects at 4.
This way, black's cor-
ner has no weakness,
and black is favored.

**Diagram 11**

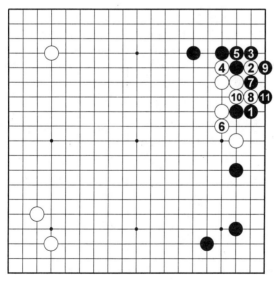

**Diagram 12 -
Black Is Better Off**
When black descends
to 1, white attacks
with sente at 2 and 4,
before extending to 6.
Black then cuts off a
stone with 7 and after
11, black solidifies a
big corner and is
better off.

**Diagram 12**

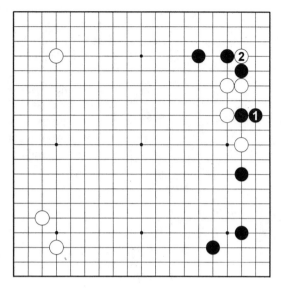

**Diagram 13**

## Diagram 13 -
## An Interesting
## Attachment

White 2 in reply to the descent of black 1 is an interesting probing attachment. In sacrificing 2, white hopes to stop the connection between the two black stones and the upper right corner.

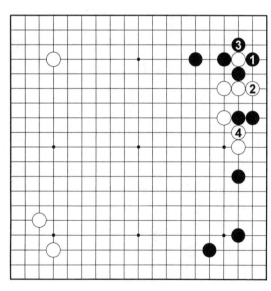

**Diagram 14**

## Diagram 14 -
## White's Intention

Black's atari at 1 is what white hopes for. After white descends to 2, black is forced to capture at 3. If black neglects 3, white descends to 3 and black is in trouble. When white hits at 4, the two black stones are dead. This shows the effect of white's probing attachment at 2 in the previous diagram.

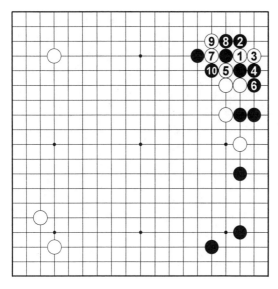

**Diagram 15**

### Diagram 15 - Black's Powerful Descent

Black's atari at 2 is the correct direction. When white descends to 3, black 4 is a powerful descent. However, the cut at white 5 is too greedy. Black nicely connects at 6. Despite white's pursuits at 7 and 9, he can't make up his losses. After black cuts at 10, white has no follow up.

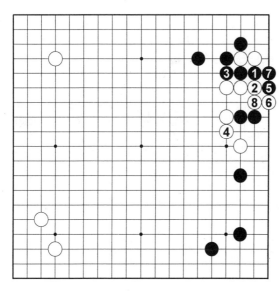

**Diagram 16**

### Diagram 16 - White Is Settled

In light of the result in the previous diagram, white calmly descends at 2 instead of cutting at 3. After black connects at 3, white takes control of the two black stones as compensation for his loss in the corner. White can be proud of being able to settle his group within black's area of influence.

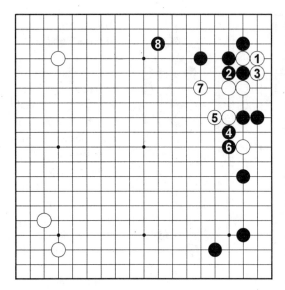

**Diagram 17**

## Diagram 17 - Black Is Better Off

Black's connection at 2 following white's descent to 1 will spoil white's plan in the previous diagram. White's connection at 3 is unavoidable. Black's hane at 4 is precalculated. With the sequence from 5 to 8, black successfully settles both his upper and lower groups.

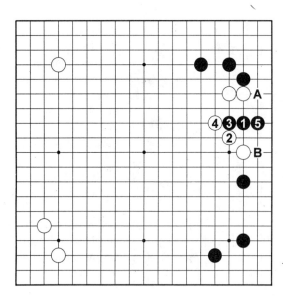

**Diagram 18**

## Diagram 18 - Ideal For black

White 2 and 4 are not powerful counter measures in reply to black's invasion at 1. Black's coolheaded descent at 5 aims to connect at either **A** or **B**. In addition, it's not easy for white to repair his weak links.

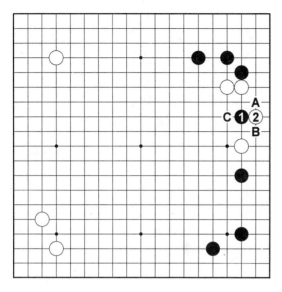

**Diagram 19 -
A Common
Attachment**
White's attachment at
2 in reply to black's
invasion at 1 is com-
mon. The objective of
2 is to connect from
either side. In reply to
white 2, black can an-
swer at either **A**, **B**, or
**C**.

Diagram 19

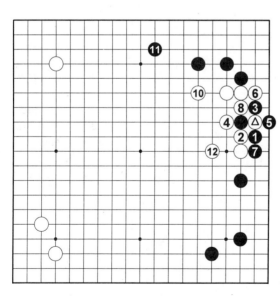

**Diagram 20 -
Probable Responses
From Both Sides**
The sequence from 1
to 9 shows the correct
play order. Realizing
that there are no ko
threats in the begin-
ning of the game,
black's connection at
9 is correct. White is
forced to reinforce at
10, although he is not
happy with the re-
sponse of black 11.
White then jumps out
to 12.

Diagram 20   (9@Δ)

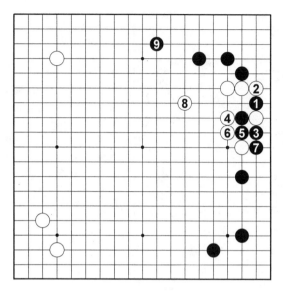

**Diagram 21**

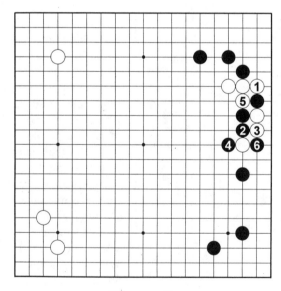

**Diagram 22**

## Diagram 21 - Both Sides Are Satisfied

White 2 is an urgent point after black hanes at 1. When black ataris at 3, white attaches at 4. Both sides are satisfied with the result of the sequence from 5 to 9. However, black can do better.

## Diagram 22 - Black Is Favored

Black's hit at 2 in reply to white's descent to 1 is correct in this situation. White is forced to extend to 3 and black hanes at 4 as planned. When white ataris at 5, black counter ataris at 6. This result favors black since white's shape is not perfect.

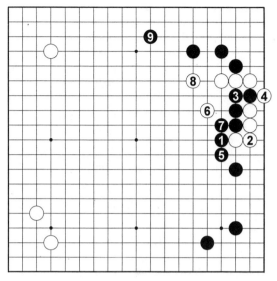

**Diagram 23 -
Black Is Solid**
If white connects at 2 in reply to black's hane at 1, black connects at 3. White settles his shape with 6 and 8. After 9, black is solid.

Diagram 23

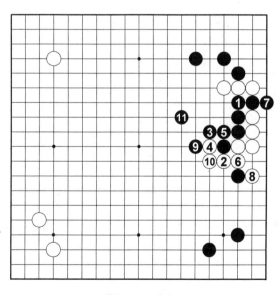

**Diagram 24 -
White Collapses**
If white hanes at 2 instead when black connects at 1, black tigers at 3 as planned. This does not favor white. The most white can do is to atari at 4 before connecting at 6. However, black's separation of white at 7 is painful for white. White collapses after black 11.

Diagram 24

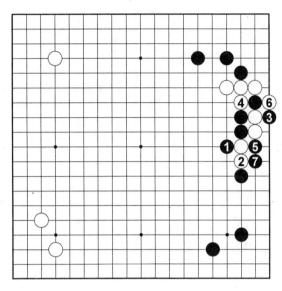

**Diagram 25 - Black's Ladder Is Favorable**

Black hanes at 1 and white hits at 2. The first line hane at 3 offers many options. After white captures at 4 and 6, black traps white with a ladder.

**Diagram 25**

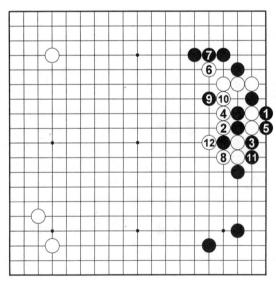

**Diagram 26 - White's Ladder Blocker**

However, to avoid the negative results of **Diagram 25**, white has the exquisite cut at 2 to avoid the ladder. Black captures two white stones with 3 and 5. White captures a black stone with the sequence through 12, settling his shape. White gets the upper hand.

**Diagram 26**

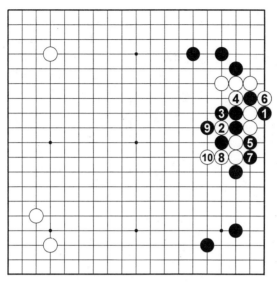

**Diagram 27 -**
**A Different Result**
After the exchange of 1 for 2, what if black ataris at 3? White captures a stone with 4 and 6, and black extends to 7. This does not favor black since the ladder does not work. Although black captures a white stone through 9, the black group is without a base.

**Diagram 27**

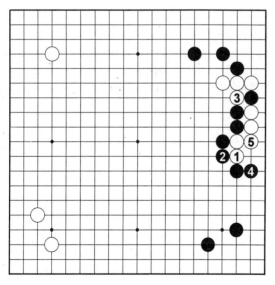

**Diagram 28 -**
**A Common But**
**Exquisite Descent**
When white hits at 1, instead of at 2 as in **Diagram 23,** black patiently blocks at 2. After white ataris at 3, black descends to 4 and can be satisfied. White is forced to connect at 5 forming an over concentrated shape. White suffers.

**Diagram 28**

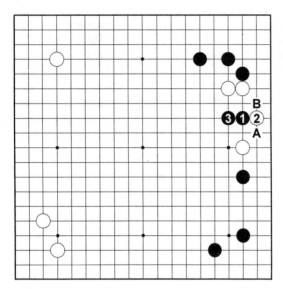

Diagram 29

## Diagram 29 - A Clumsy Extension

Blacks's extension to 3 after the exchange of 1 and 2 is clumsy. However, the result depends on white's reply. Therefore white should be careful in choosing between **A** or **B** for his reply.

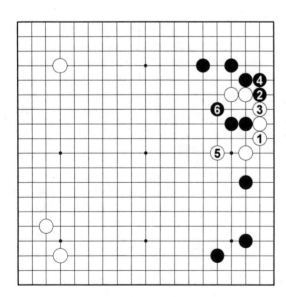

Diagram 30

## Diagram 30 - Black Is Better Off

If white extends to 1, the hane at 2 and the connection at 4 are urgent shape points. Black secures the corner and takes away white's base with 2 and 4. If white jumps towards the center at 5, then black diagonals at 6 sealing off two white stones. This favors black.

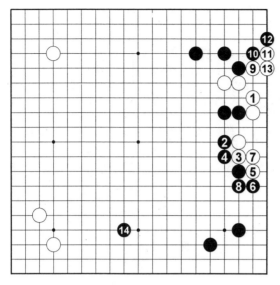

Diagram 31

**Diagram 31 -
Clear Cut Outward
Influence**
White's drawback to 1
is the correct choice.
Black confines white
with the urgent point
at 2. White 3 and 5
are crude plays in that
they help black make
thickness. Black seals
white off with sente at
6 and 8. White is
worse off.

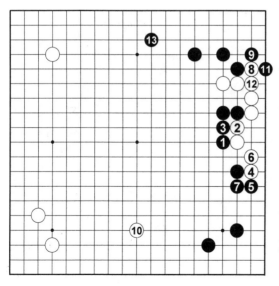

Diagram 32

**Diagram 32 -
Diametrically
Opposing Plays**
White's hit at 2 fol-
lowing black's press
at 1, and the attach-
ment at 4 following
the connection at 3 is
the correct play order.
The sequence through
7 is inevitable. With
sente, white occupies
the big territorial point
at 10. On the other
hand, black ataris at
11, before jumping to
13. Both sides play
diametrically opposite.

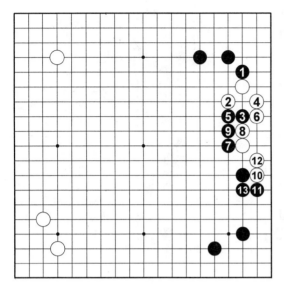

Diagram 33

**Diagram 33 -**
**White Suffers**
White's diagonal at 2 in reply to black's hit at 1 is not good. The purpose of white 2 is to discourage black from invading. Comparing this result to that of **Diagram 32** clearly shows that white is worse off here.

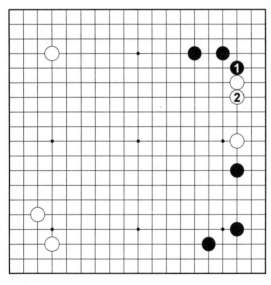

Diagram 34

**Diagram 34 -**
**A Super Slack**
**Drawback**
White's drawback to 2 in reply to black 1 forms an unfavorable shape. This yields too much and white has to work even harder to catch up.

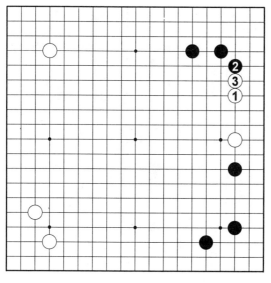

Diagram 35

## Diagram 35 - Analysis

Let's analyze why white 2 in the previous diagram is not good. White's two-space extension to 1 is a common tactic used to settle one's group. Black's diagonal at 2 is excellent for securing the corner territory and attacking white. White's extension to 3 is terrible at this juncture. By the same token, white 2 in **Diagram 34** is also bad.

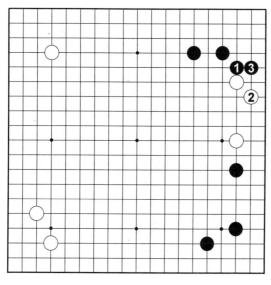

Diagram 36

## Diagram 36 - White Is Thin

Some may consider a diagonal at 2 in reply to black 1. Black is solid after descending to 3. In contrast, white is thin.

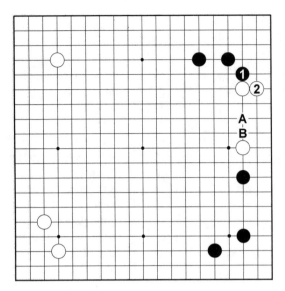

**Diagram 37**

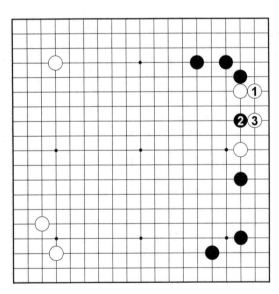

**Diagram 38**

**Diagram 37 -**
**A Powerful Descent**
White's descent to 2 is powerful. Black can either invade at **A**, or attach at **B**.

**Diagram 38 -**
**Black Gets Nothing**
Black 2 seems to be an urgent point in reply to White's descent at 1. However, white aims to connect to either side by attaching at 3. As a result, black gets nothing. Although the position of white 1 is on the second line, it effectively prevents an invasion.

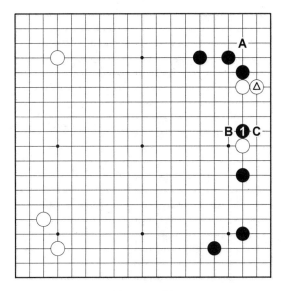

**Diagram 39 -
A Black Tesuji**
Black's attachment at 1 is a tesuji in answer to the descent at Δ. This is also the sequence used in the actual game. White can answer at either **A**, **B**, or **C**.

Diagram 39

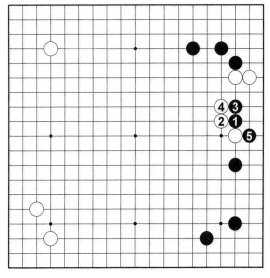

**Diagram 40 -
Black's Intention**
Black's attachment at 1 lures white to press at 2. Black then extends to 3 with sente and hanes at 5, to take away white's base. White should have adopted other tactics to prevent his group from floating without a base.

Diagram 40

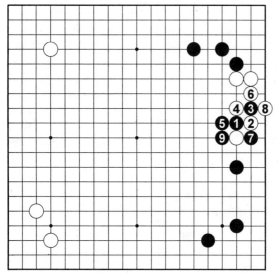

**Diagram 41**

### Diagram 41 - An Ugly Shape

If white hanes at 2 instead, black's two-step hane at 3 is a tesuji. White captures a black stone with the sequence through 8. However, when black ataris at 9, white ends up with an over concentrated shape.

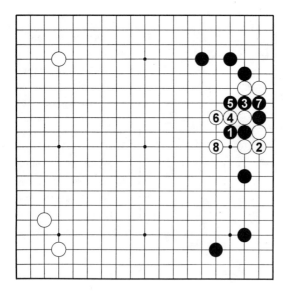

**Diagram 42**

### Diagram 42 - Black's Territory Is Large

What if white 6 in the previous diagram connects at 2 instead? Black sacrifices two stones with ataris at 3 and 5 and secures a large corner. Although white gains some outward influence, the value of black's corner outweighs white's gain.

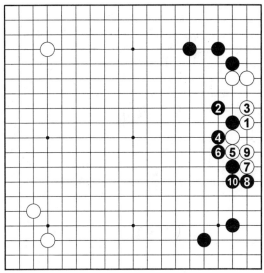

**Diagram 43**

### Diagram 43 - Black Is Thick

Black can also consider a diagonal at 2 in reply to white's hane at 1. Black 2 is a powerful tactic for building outside influence. The sequence from white's extension to 3, to black's connection at 10 is inevitable. From a global point of view, black is thick.

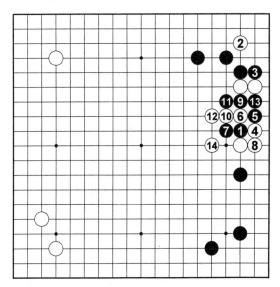

**Diagram 44**

### Diagram 44 - Sacrifice Tactics

When black attaches at 1, white invades at 3-3 to create potential by sacrificing stones. If black blocks at 3, white hanes at 4. The sequence from 5 to 14 forms the same result as in **Diagram 42**. However, with the presence of white 2, black's corner is weak.

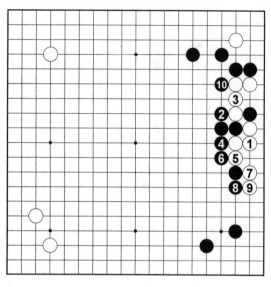

**Diagram 45**

## Diagram 45 - Black's Thickness

After white connects at 1, black can use sacrifice tactics with an atari at 2 (instead of the atari at 9 in **Diagram 44**). It will be difficult for white to come out ahead. Black allows white to secure a small territory with the sequence from 4 to 10. However, black creates overwhelming outward influence which clearly favors black.

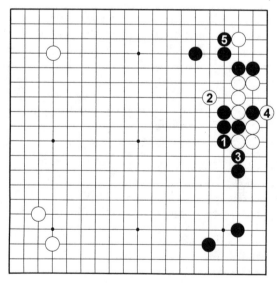

**Diagram 46**

## Diagram 46 - Securing Both Groups

If white jumps to 2 (instead of extending to 5 in **Diagram 45**), to seek variation, black hits with momentum at 3. White ataris at 4 to settle his group. After the block at 5, black successfully secures both of his groups.

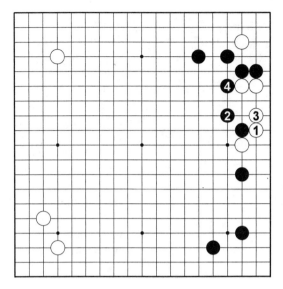

## Diagram 47 - An Urgent Point For Black's Shape

When white hanes at 1, black's diagonal at 2 should also work. Black 2 prompts white to extend to 3, before making a tiger at 4. Black 4 is an urgent point for black's shape, and it is also a hane at the head of two white stones.

Diagram 47

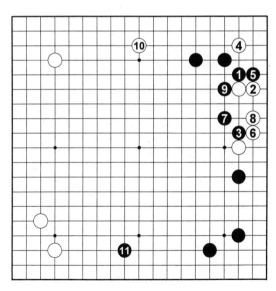

## Diagram 48 - Actual Game

In the actual game, when black attaches at 3, white picks the best replies at 4 and 6. The diagonal at 7 is good style with aji. Black completely seals off white after 9, reflecting the success of the novel attachment. In conclusion, white 2 in reply to 1 is questionable. Black won the game by 12.5 points after 259 plays.

Diagram 48

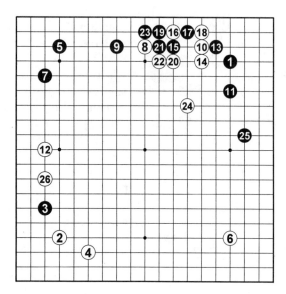

**Diagram 49**

**Diagram 49 -**
**Example 1 (1-26)**
This example is taken from the quarter final of the 25th Myung-in Tournament. Kim Song-ryong 3 dan took black against Choe Myong-hun 3 dan. After white 14, black invades at 15. The sequence through white 24 is inevitable. White won the game by 4.5 points after 225 plays.

**Diagram 50**

**Diagram 50 -**
**Example 2 (1-23)**
This example is taken from the third game of the 33rd Highest Ranking Tournament (Chaigowi). Lee Changho 6 dan took black against Cho Hunhyun 9 dan. Black won by resignation after 159 plays.

# Chapter Six
## An Extraordinary Novel Jump

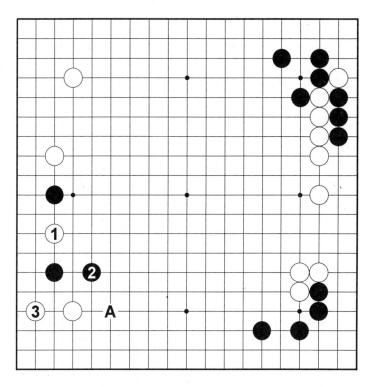

**Example 6**

This is the seventh game of the fourth Korean Kisung Tournament. Lee Changho takes white against Cho Hunhyun. Lee and Cho were tied 3-3 and it all boiled down to this final game of the biggest tournament in Korea. At that time, nobody could predict who would capture the crown. In this game, Lee played an extraordinary jump which led to novel plays that gained an unexpected victory for him. After white invaded at 1 and black jumped to 2, white made the extraordinary jump to 3 instead of the normal jump to **A**. Let us analyze the position as follows.

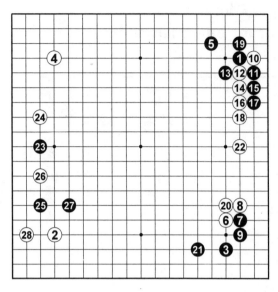

**Diagram 1**

## Diagram 1 -
## Actual Game

Black 1, 3, and 5 are a typical fuseki which stresses real territory. When black draws back to 9, white is not eager to settle the local shape on the lower right corner but probes black's position at 10 instead. Most people think that white is thick after white 20. Black splits the left side with 23. When black jumps to 27, white 28 is a novel jump in reply.

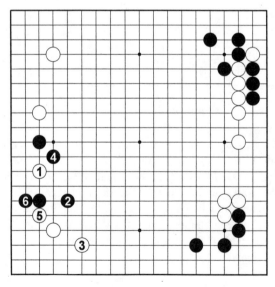

**Diagram 2**

## Diagram 2 -
## Traditional
## Response

White's invasion at 1 is a common sophisticated tactic for settling his shape with the sacrifice of white 1. Black 2 through 6 is a basic position which frequently appears in actual games. The advantage is that white gets sente; the disadvantage is that the door is still open in the corner.

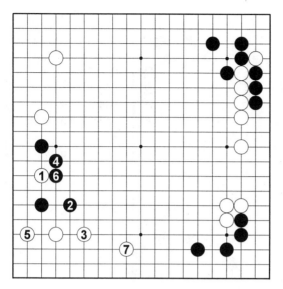

**Diagram 3 -
A Variation**
Due to the unsatisfactory open door in the previous diagram, white could extend at 3 and defend the corner by jumping to 5, securing real territory. However, since white has to defend at 7 after black 6, white loses sente.

**Diagram 3**

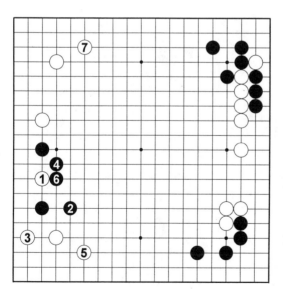

**Diagram 4 -
White's Intention**
After the exchange of 1 and 2, white 3 intends to let black 4 capture a stone. White then jumps to 5 taking the corner with sente. When black reinforces at 6, white takes the upper left corner with 7, capturing a big territorial point on the top.

**Diagram 4**

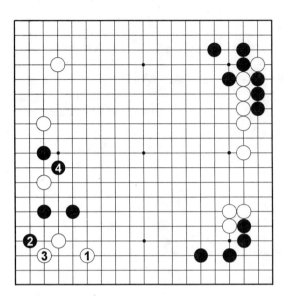

**Diagram 5**

### Diagram 5 - White's Perception

If white simply jumps to 1, black jumps into the corner at 2. After white defends at 3, black surrounds a white stone with 4. White's obvious dissatisfaction with this result, led to the creation of the novel jump.

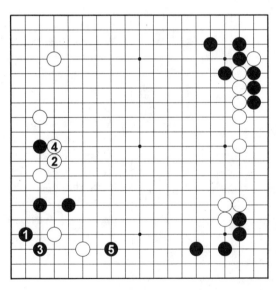

**Diagram 6**

### Diagram 6 - White's Counterattack

When black jumps into the corner at 1, he anticipates white will diagonal with 2 at 3 (**Diagram 5**). However, white's counterattack at 2 gains momentum. Both sides stabilize with 3 and 4. Black then takes the initiative by attacking white with the pincer at 5.

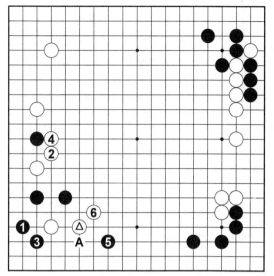

**Diagram 7**

**Diagram 7 -**
**An Elastic Shape**
If Δ is the one space jump instead of **A**, black's jump to 1 is not good. The sequence from 2 to 5 is exactly identical to that of the previous diagram. However, with the high position of Δ, white has a more elastic shape with the diagonal at 6.

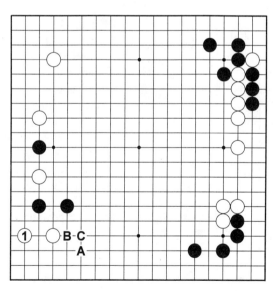

**Diagram 8**

**Diagram 8 -**
**The Next Play**
White defends the corner by jumping to 1 with sente. In order not to fall into white's trap, black needs to select the next play from either **A**, **B**, or **C**.

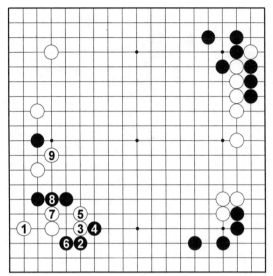

**Diagram 9 -
Unfavorable For
Black**

Black's attack at 2 is
an overplay. White
presses at 3 and natu-
rally pushes through at
5 dividing black and
attacking both black
groups.

Diagram 9

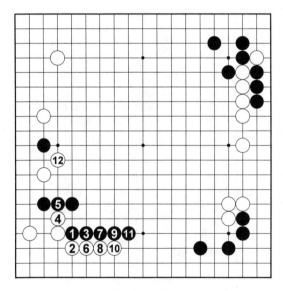

**Diagram 10 -
A Fast-paced White
Handles Situation**

If black attaches at 1,
white hanes at 2. Af-
ter black extends to 3,
white severely thrusts
with sente at 4. White
handles the situation
with a fast pace from
6 to 10, before occu-
pying the key point at
12. The position fa-
vors white.

Diagram 10

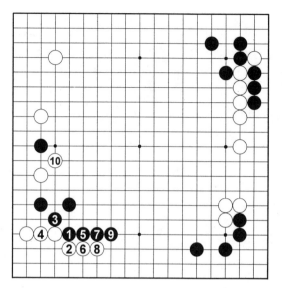

**Diagram 11**

## Diagram 11 - A Similar Result

If black answers at 3, white connects at 4. Black still loses sente with the sequence through 9 and allows white to capture the vital point at 10. Similar to the previous diagram, this is not favorable for black.

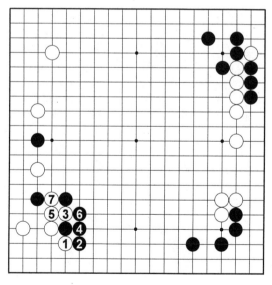

**Diagram 12**

## Diagram 12 - Big Territory for White

If black hanes at 2 instead, white ataris at 3 and connects at 5, forcing black to block at 6. After white pokes through at 7, white's territory in the corner is big. Since black's position is low on the lower right corner, the outward influence black constructed with the sequence to 6 is not so valuable.

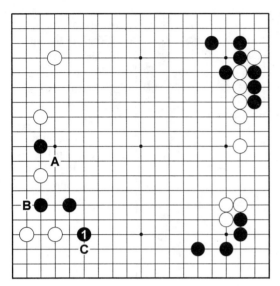

**Diagram 13 -**
**Sealing Tactics**
The tactic of sealing white in with 1 is correct. White can consider responding at **A**, **B**, or **C**.

**Diagram 13**

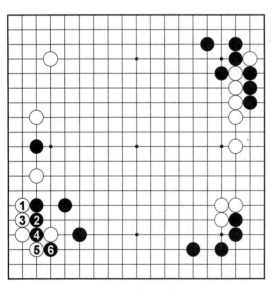

**Diagram 14 -**
**White is Submissive**
White's attachment at 1 is too submissive. Although white manages to connect with 3, black reaps profit with 4 and 6. This is not acceptable for white.

**Diagram 14**

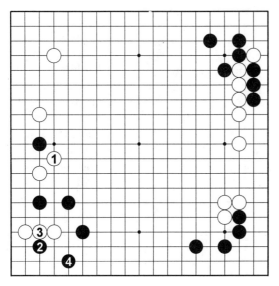

**Diagram 15**

**Diagram 15 - Entering White's Corner**

If white diagonals at 1, black jumps into white's corner with a peep at 2. After white connects at 3, black jumps to 4 with excellent shape. On the other hand, white still needs to reinforce his shape.

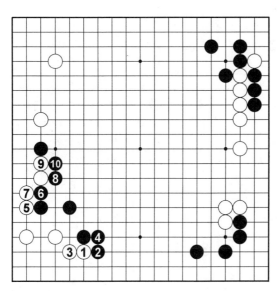

**Diagram 16**

**Diagram 16 - Black's Outward Influence Is Tremendous**

If white attaches at 1, the drawback to 3 is sente. White then pushes along the second line at 5 and 7, linking up with his lone stone. However, this allows black to build up tremendous outward influence which favors black.

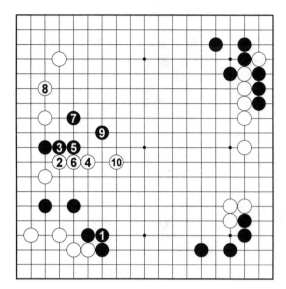

Diagram 17

### Diagram 17 - Splitting Attack

When black connects at 1, white 2 is a vital point which prevents black from connecting underneath on the second line. The development towards the center with the sequence through 10 is inevitable. This is the best result for both sides.

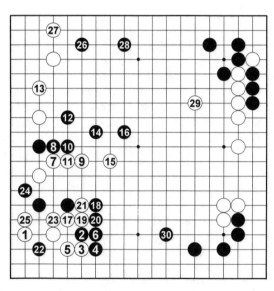

Diagram 18

### Diagram 18 - Actual Game

The novel jump led to a ferocious battle in the lower left corner. Black 22 and 24 are exquisite shape and link attacks. The game ended with 252 plays and white winning by 8.5 points.

# Chapter Seven
# A Dominating Novel Knight by a Young Player

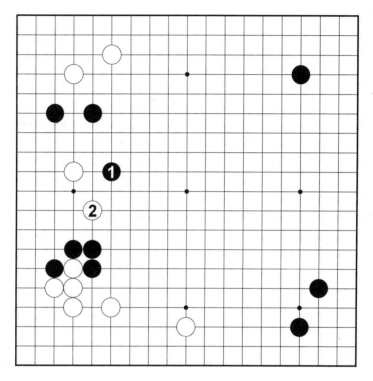

**Example 7**

This game is from the second round of the 33rd Highest Ranking (Chaigowi) Tournament. Yun Song-hyon 3 dan, known as one of the four top innovative players in Korea, took white against Chong Hyon-san 4 dan. Due to the nature of this tournament, novel plays are readily manifested. However, unlike most novel plays, the knight jump at 2 is quite creative. After the game, analyses from all sources indicated that this novel knight jump is very powerful. Now, let's analyze the attack and defense aspects which evolve from this novel knight.

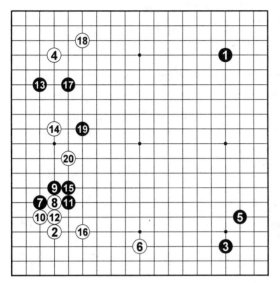

**Diagram 1**

## Diagram 1 - Actual Game

White's attachment at 8 and tiger at 10 are a powerful maneuver to secure the corner territory following black's approach at 7. When black approaches again at 13, white tries to complicate the situation with a pincer at 14. Black then caps at 19 and white knight jumps to 20.

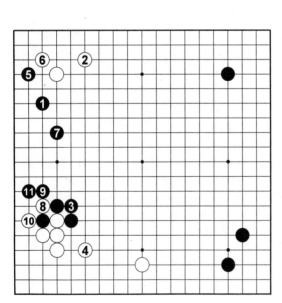

**Diagram 2**

## Diagram 2 - Black Settles His Shape

If white patiently extends at 2, the sequence from 3 to 11 is the most common development and allows black to easily settle his group on the left. Therefore, it's better for white to adopt the tactics in the previous diagram.

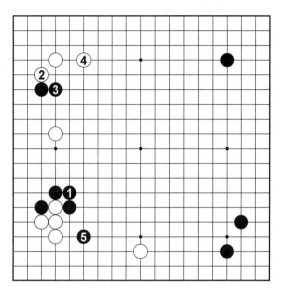

**Diagram 3**

### Diagram 3 - White Is Greedy

If white greedily defends at 2 and 4 on the upper left corner in reply to black's connection at 1 (black 15 in **Diagram 1**), black's jump to 5 is the best maneuver to punish white. White is in a difficult position.

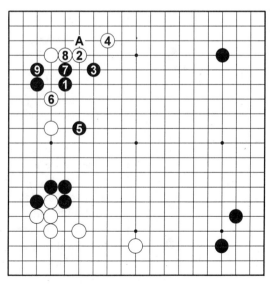

**Diagram 4**

### Diagram 4 - One Space Difference

Although it's only a one space difference, white reinforcing at 2 instead of **A** of **Diagram 3** may create problems for white. Black's press at 3 is a strong attack against the upper side. When white reinforces at 4, black solidifies his shape with 7 and 9. This makes it difficult for white to handle his group on the left.

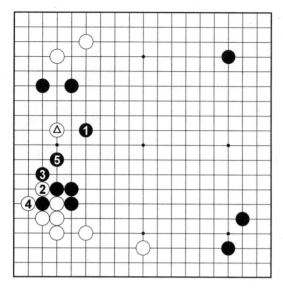

**Diagram 6**

## Diagram 5 - White Is Not Satisfied

When black caps at 1, white makes the mistake of capturing a black stone with 2 and 4 instead of rescuing Δ. Black ataris at 3 and tigers at 5 and is allowed to settle his group in what was white's hemisphere of influence. White is not satisfied.

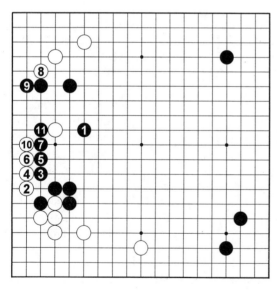

**Diagram 6**

## Diagram 6 - A Diametrically Opposed Position

If white insists on maneuvering on this side, 2 is the urgent point. After black presses at 3, white gets real territory with sente with the sequence through 10. White 8 is an alert defense obtaining profit with sente. On the other hand, in taking control of a white stone, black can be satisfied too. A diametrically opposed position results.

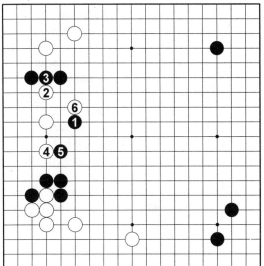

**Diagram 7 - Conventional Development**

After the exchange of 2 for 3, white's jump to 4 is conventional. Black then presses at 5 and white tries to break through at 6.

**Diagram 7**

**Diagram 8 - White Is Favored**

The hane at 1 is standard. White then attaches at 2, intending to cut black apart. With the sequence through 10, black is split into two groups. White is slightly favored as compared to black.

**Diagram 8**

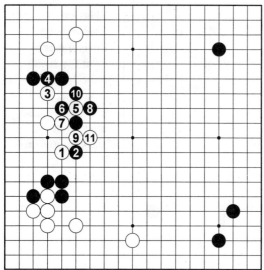

Diagram 9

### Diagram 9 -
### White Is Successful

If white jumps to 1, black blocks at 2. White's counter atari at 9 following black's atari at 8 is severe. White sacrifices one stone and is successful in pushing through and splitting black into two groups with the sequence through 11.

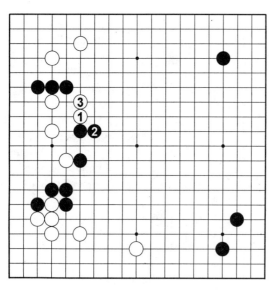

Diagram 9

### Diagram 1 0 -
### White Is Better off

Black's extension to 2 in reply to white 1 is even worse for black. White's extension at 3 is a strong reinforcement, making it difficult for black to reply. Therefore, black should not maneuver this way.

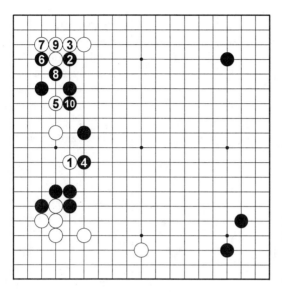

**Diagram 11**

**Diagram 11 -
Taking Advantage
Alertly**
Following **Diagram 1**
black's probe at 2 in
reply to white 1 is
very interesting. After
white reinforces at 3,
black presses at 4.
When white peeps at
5, black 6 and 8 are a
precalculated attack to
reap profit. Black
seals at 10 with sente
and is successful with
this variation.

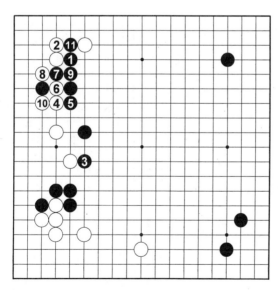

**Diagram 12**

**Diagram 12 -
Black's Outward
Influence**
To avoid the result of
the previous diagram,
white extends to 2.
When white peeps at
4, black's block at 5
from the center is cru-
cial. Black's wedge at
7 and the connection
at 9 are tesujis in reply
to white's poke at 6.
White ataris at 10 and
black's thrust at 11
forms overwhelming
outward influence.

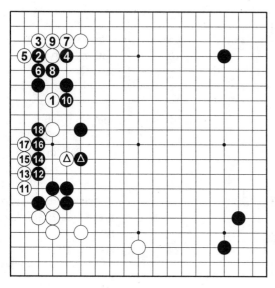

**Diagram 13**

## Diagram 13 - Best Development For Both Sides

After the exchange of △ and ▲, black probes white at 2 in reply to white's peep at 1. White reinforces at 3 and with the sequence through 8, black's sente attack gains profit, before the key block at 10. On the other hand, white 11 thru 17 flexibly make use of his sacrifice stones. This is the best development for both sides.

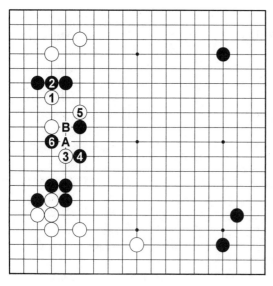

**Diagram 14**

## Diagram 14 - Correct Play Order

Jumping to white 3 after the exchange of white 1 for black 2 is the correct order. The attachment at black 6 is a tesuji. White can now choose to reply at **A** or **B**.

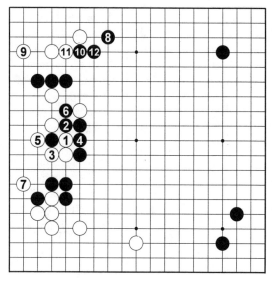

**Diagram 15 -**
**Black Is Thick**
The sequence to 7, following white's poke at 1, is the correct play order. With the help of his center influence, black blocks at 8. White 9 is a solid defense. After attaching at 10 and drawing back to 12, black's outward influence is thick without any weaknesses.

**Diagram 15**

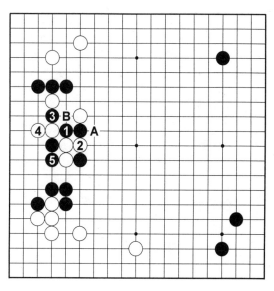

**Diagram 16 -**
**Difficult For White**
White's poke at 2, instead of an atari at 5 in reply to black 1, is unreasonable. Black attacks white with an atari at 3 and an extension to 5. If white ataris at **A**, black connects at **B**, making it difficult for White.

**Diagram 16**

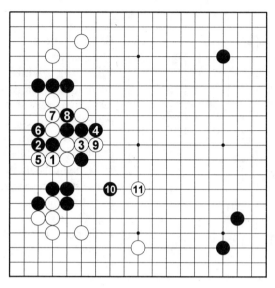

**Diagram 17**

## Diagram 17 -
## Black Is In A Passive Defensive Position

On the other hand, it is unreasonable for black to escape when white ataris at 1. Although black manages to rescue his stones, the life and death status of the black dragon on the lower left is questionable. If black tries to escape by jumping to 10, white pursues at 11, putting black in a passive defensive position.

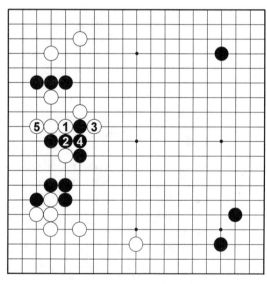

**Diagram 18**

## Diagram 18 -
## Another Variation

What if white hits at 1 instead of poking at 2? When black connects at 2, white's atari at 3 is sente. White then descends to 5, splitting black into two pieces. Now, how does black handle his three stones on the upper left?

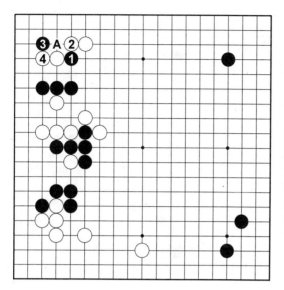

Diagram 19

### Diagram 19 - Exquisite Sabaki

Black's probing attachment at 1 is a very effective sabaki. After white blocks at 2, the peep at black 3 was preplanned. Although white resists stubbornly with a block at 4, black can turn the tide by making use of white's weakness at **A**.

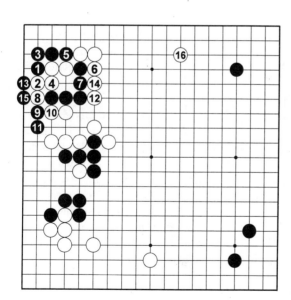

Diagram 20

### Diagram 20 - Even Exchange

Continuing from the previous diagram, black's hane at 1 is the urgent point for shape. After white 2 and 4, black cuts at 5. Although black beats white by one liberty with the sequence from 6 to 15, white sacrifices his stones for outward influence, and he can be satisfied after he jumps to 16.

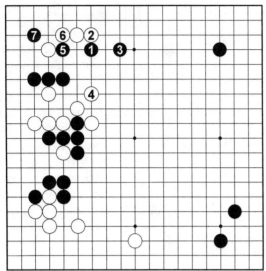

**Diagram 21 -
A More Powerful
Maneuver**

Black's shoulder hit at
1 instead of attaching
at 5 is more powerful.
After white 4, it is
important to attach at
5. The plan for the
white 6 and black 7
maneuvers is similar
to the previous dis-
cussion in **Diagram
19**.

**Diagram 21**

**Diagram 22 -
Black Succeeds**

Continuing from the
previous diagram, the
sequence through
white 8 is identical to
that of **Diagram 20**.
Black's connection at
9 is the key now. Af-
ter white connects at
10, black tigers at 11,
trapping three white
stones and is better
off.

**Diagram 22**

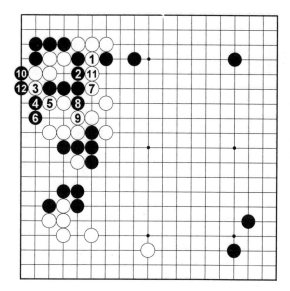

Diagram 23

## Diagram 23 -
## Black Is Favored

If white ataris at 1 and extends at 3, then black beats white by one liberty with the sequence from 4 to 12. Black's position has more vitality than that of **Diagram 20**. White is worse off.

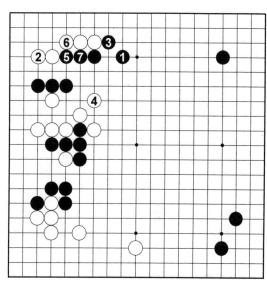

Diagram 24

## Diagram 24 -
## Black Is Thick

When black jumps to 1, if white defends the corner at 2, black tigers at 3. After white reinforces at 4, black is thick after connecting at 5 and 7.

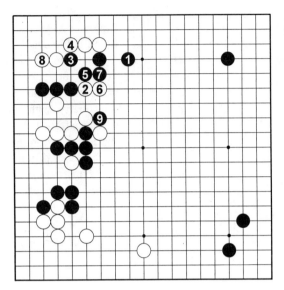

**Diagram 25**

## Diagram 25 - Difficult For White

White's counterattack at 2 in reply to black's shoulder hit at 1 is unreasonable. Although the shape of black 3, 5 and 7 is not that desirable, it is the correct maneuver for attacking white. After white reinforces at 8, black's cut at 9 makes it difficult for white.

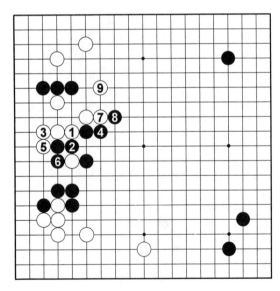

**Diagram 26**

## Diagram 26 - Not Exploiting The Option Of Atari

After the exchange of 1 and 2, white extends to 3 instead of an atari at 4. When black extends to 4, white turns to 5 with sente. The sequence through 9 is inevitable. The question is how should black handle his three stones on the upper left.

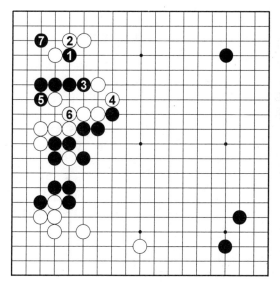

Diagram 27

**Diagram 27 -
Using White's
Weakness In The
Corner**
Continuing from the previous diagram, black can rescue his three stones by using white's weakness in the corner. The attachment at black 1 is the first step. After white blocks at 2, black reaps profit with sente at 3 and 5 before the planned peep at 7.

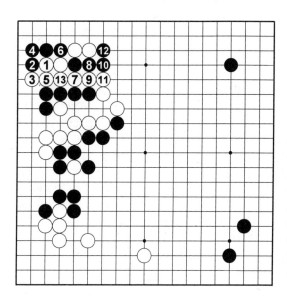

Diagram 28

**Diagram 28 -
Sacrifice Strategy**
When white blocks at 1, black's hane and connection at 2 and 4 are correct. White traps five black stones with the sequence through 13. On the other hand, black traps two white stones and obtains profit in the corner with sente. As a result, black's sacrifice strategy is successful.

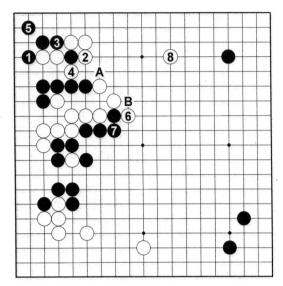

**Diagram 29**

Diagram 29 -
**Cutting Points In White's Shape**
After black's hane at 1 and white's atari at 2, black's cut at 3 is crucial. The sequence through 5 is the only order. White ataris at 6 with sente and jumps to 8. The cutting points at **A** and **B** do not favor White.

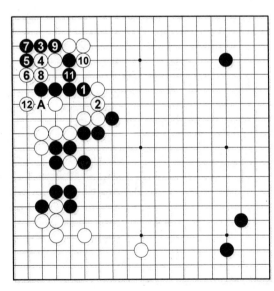

**Diagram 30**

Diagram 30 -
**Black Is Annihilated**
After black hits at 1, white connects at 2 instead of making a tiger. This prevents black from taking advantage at **A**. Black's peep at 3 is what white wants. White ataris at 10 and jumps to 12, annihilating black.

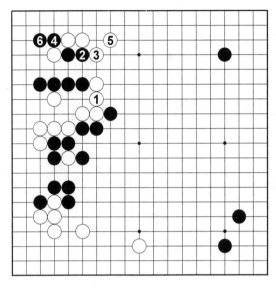

Diagram 31

**Diagram 31 -
An Urgent Point In
Shape**
Black's extension at 2
in reply to white's
connection at 1 is an
urgent point to fix his
shape. After white 3,
black cuts at 4 and
occupies the corner
with 6. The position
favors black.

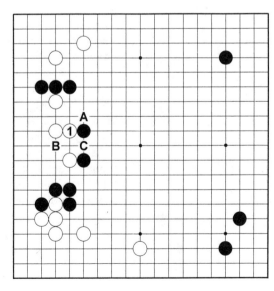

Diagram 32

**Diagram 32 -
Another Variation**
White's attachment at
**A** for linking to the
center will lead to ad-
verse effects because
of black's attachment
at **B**. Therefore, white
hits at 1 instead.
Black can consider
extending at **A** or connecting at **C**.

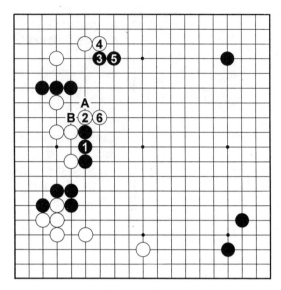

**Diagram 33**

## Diagram 33 - White Succeeds

Black's connection at 1 is slack. When white hanes at 2, black has no follow up. A black hane at 6 will certainly prompt white to extend to **A**. Therefore, black shoulder hits at 3 instead. White's extension at 6 reinforces his weakness at **B** and white is successful.

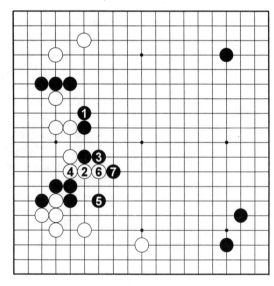

**Diagram 34**

## Diagram 34 - Variation Of Black's Extension

Black can also extend to 1. White tries to cut black in two with the hane at 2. Black strongly counterattacks with 3 to 7. White has to be careful here. One wrong play will lead to total defeat.

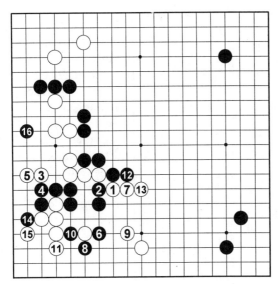

**Diagram 35**

**Diagram 35 -**
**Difficult For White**
Following the previous diagram, white's hane at 1 attacking black's dragon is very unreasonable. Both sides make the best plays from 2 to 16. Even if white manages to make life, white's territory is destroyed and this does not favor white.

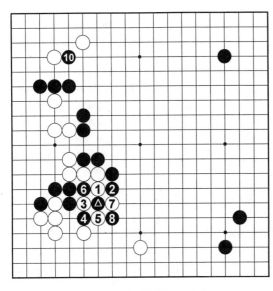

**Diagram 36  (9@3, 11@▲)**

**Diagram 36 -**
**A Giant Ko**
Although the turn at 1 and wedge at 3 result in bad shape for white, it is a tesuji. A ko is formed with the sequence through 8. After white captures the ko stone with sente, black ko threats at 10. Realizing that this is a giant ko, white connects at 11, killing the black dragon.

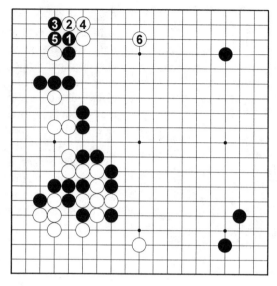

Diagram 37

### Diagram 37 -
### Price Of Ignoring A Ko Threat

Black tries to make up for the difference of having his dragon captured by securing the upper left corner with 1 to 5. However, this is not enough. White lightly jumps to 6 and still has the lead.

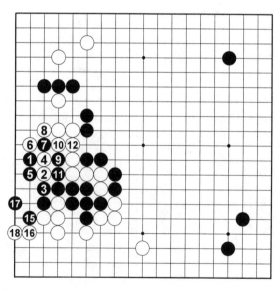

Diagram 38    (13@7, 14@4)

### Diagram 38 -
### Black Is One Liberty Short

In **Diagram 36**, if black 8 connects at 3 and white 9 connects at 8, then the purpose of black 1 here is to start a capturing race. However, after white peeps at 2, black still falls short. Black resists to the greatest extent from 3 to 17 but white beats black by one liberty after 18.

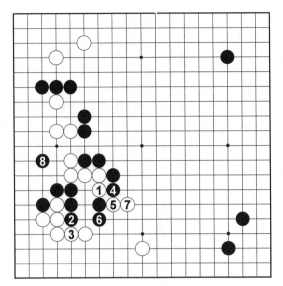

**Diagram 39 -
White Dies**
After white extends at
1, black thrusts at 2
before blocking at 4.
When white cuts at 5,
black's extension at 6
is coolheaded. White
extends to 7 and black
jumps to 8, killing the
white dragon.

**Diagram 39**

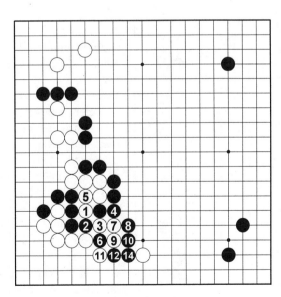

**Diagram 40 -
Sacrificing Stones
For Outward
Influence**
If white cuts at 1 in-
stead of at 5 in **Dia-
gram 39**, black blocks
at 2. When white
ataris at 3, black's
connection at 4 is
solid. After white
captures six black
stones with 5, black
builds up over-
whelming outward
influence from 6 to
14. Black's sacrifice
tactics are successful.

**Diagram 40  (13@6)**

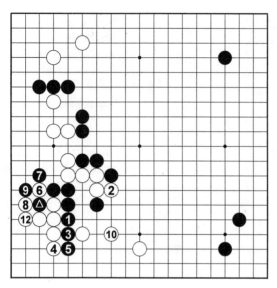

Diagram 41 (11@▲)

## Diagram 41 - Unpredictable Outcome

White's thrust at 2 is a basic defense in reply to 1. Black thrusts with momentum at 3 and 5. The sequence from 4 through 12 is the best play order. The outcome is difficult to predict.

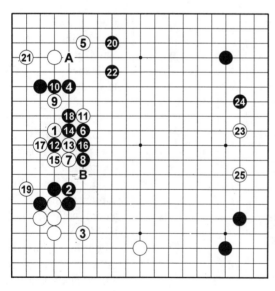

Diagram 42

## Diagram 42 - Actual Game

White should have peeped at 9 and waited for black to connect at 10 before jumping to 7. On the other hand, black should not have connected at 10, in reply to white's peep at 9, but should have attached at **A** instead to probe white. Both sides played in diametrically opposite ways in the sequence through 22. White has the threat to hane at **B** in the future.

# Chapter Eight
# An International Championship Tournament's
# Novel Peep

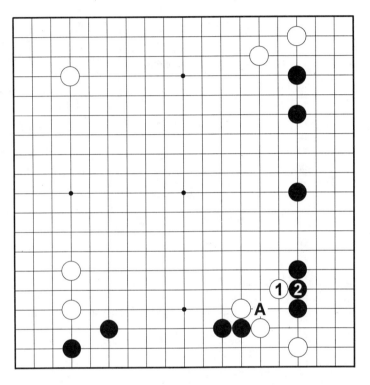

**Example 8**

This game is from the final of the 6th Fujitsu Cup Tournament. Cho Hunhyun took white against Yu Chang-hyok. White's peep at 1 prompted black's connection at 2. This novel peep has the adverse effect of helping black become strong. However, this peep also helps prevent the cut at **A**. Let's look at the attack and defense aspects of this novel peep.

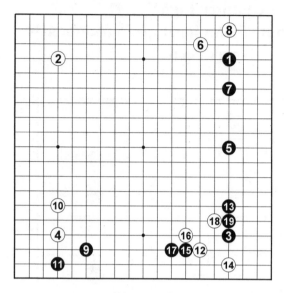

Diagram 1

### Diagram 1 - Actual Game

Black ignores white 8 and approaches the lower left corner at 9. White ignores black 11 and approaches the lower right corner at 12. These are examples of a modern fast-paced fuseki. Black 15 is currently a popular response to white 14. White 18 is the novel peep.

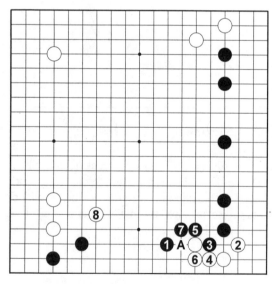

Diagram 2

### Diagram 2 - Conventional Joseki

Black 1 is a variation in place of an attachment at **A**. It's more efficient than **A** if black wants to build up outward influence. White gets territory with the sequence from 2 to 7 and black gets outward influence. This is a basic star point joseki. White's jump at 8 is an excellent point to contain black's outward influence.

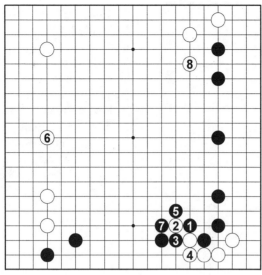

**Diagram 3 -
A White Ladder
Block**
If white hanes at 2 instead, black ataris with a ladder at 5. White then blocks the ladder at 6. After black captures at 7, black is thick. On the other hand, white jumps to 8 with a fast pace. The game proceeds conventionally.

**Diagram 3**

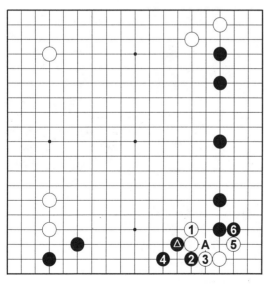

**Diagram 4 -
White Has A
Terrible Shape**
Before we analyze the novel peep, let's look at some variations of the attachment at ▲. White 1 is a very slack extension. The hane at 2 and the tiger at 4 are strong shape attacks. Due to the cut at **A**, white has to connect and ends up with a terrible shape.

**Diagram 4**

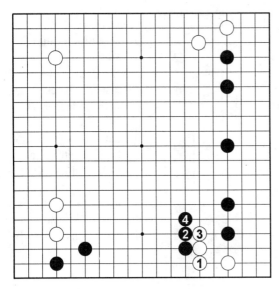

**Diagram 5**

**Diagram 5 -**
**White Is One Step**
**Behind**
The descent to 1 is bad because it creates an overconcentrated low position. With black's extensions at 2 and 4, white is always one step behind in escaping towards the center and cannot be satisfied with this line of play.

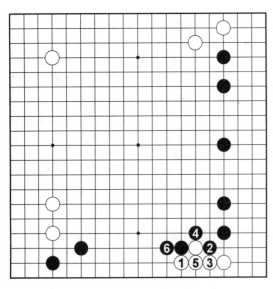

**Diagram 6**

**Diagram 6 -**
**White Is Compressed**
If white hanes at 1 instead, the clamp at 2 is a tesuji. A submissive reply at 3 will prompt black to atari at 4, compressing white on the second line. This position is not favorable for white either.

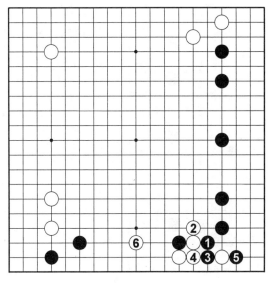

**Diagram 7 -**
**Diametrically**
**Opposed Responses**
White thrusts at 2 instead of blocking at 3 as in the previous diagram to prevent black from sealing white off. Black's descent to 3 is certain, followed by black's key attachment at 5 to defend the corner. After white jumps to 6, both sides can be satisfied.

**Diagram 7**

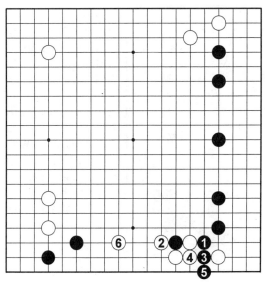

**Diagram 8 -**
**Even Exchange**
If white ataris at 2 instead, the sequence through white 6 is conceivable. The result can be considered an even exchange.

**Diagram 8**

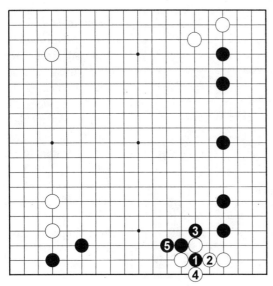

**Diagram 9**

### Diagram 9 -
### A Cutting Tesuji
When white hanes on the second line, black's cut at 1 is a tesuji for probing white. If white ataris at 2, black seals white off with 3 and 5 with sente and can be satisfied.

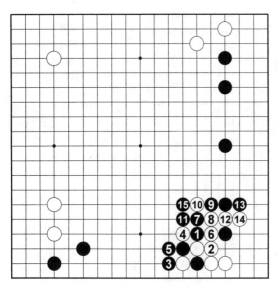

**Diagram 10**

### Diagram 10 -
### Black Builds Overwhelming Outward Influence
If white connects at 2 (instead of capturing at 4 as in the previous diagram) black counter ataris at 3. White reaps profit from 4 to 14. Using sacrifice tactics, black builds overwhelming outward influence.

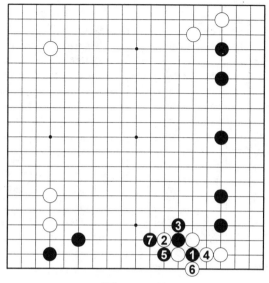

**Diagram 11**

## Diagram 11 - Depends On The Ladder

White's atari at 2 in reply to black's cut at 1 works only if the ladder favors white. Now that the ladder is favorable for black, white suffers after black 7.

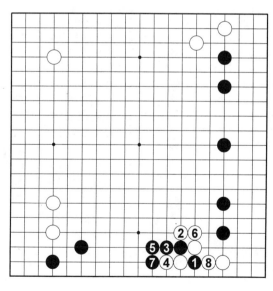

**Diagram 12**

## Diagram 12 - White Is Favored

White's atari at 2 followed by the extension at 4 is basic knowledge. Black's extension at 5 prevents a white hane. White's connection at 6 is solid. After the exchange of 7 and 8, white gets both territory and a chance to run towards the center. This definitely favors white.

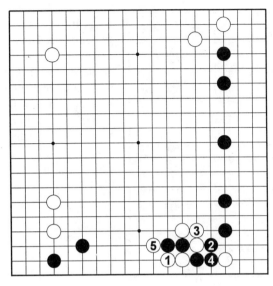

**Diagram 13**

## Diagram 13 - Even Ground

After white extends to 1 (white 4 in the previous diagram), black's atari and connection at 2 and 4 are the correct approach to secure territory in the corner. After white traps two black stones at 5, both sides are on even ground. However, as far as the deployment of stones is concerned, black is slightly favored.

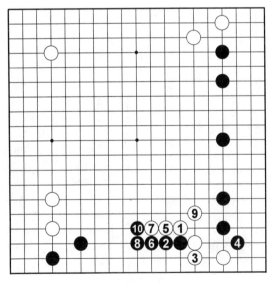

**Diagram 14**

## Diagram 14 - White Is Not Satisfied

If white descends to 3 after the exchange of 1 for 2 (16 and 17 in **Diagram 1**), black successfully settles his groups on both sides with 4 to 10. In contrast, white's shape is not complete, and white is not satisfied.

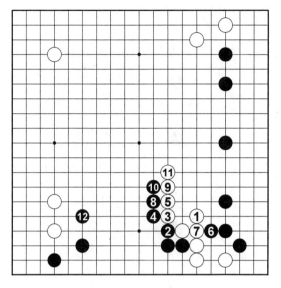

**Diagram 15 -
An Ideal Shape**
If white tigers at 1 (instead of extending to 5 in the previous diagram), black presses with 2 and 4 and forces white to extend to 5. Black then peeps with sente at 6. After white extends to 11, black jumps to 12 and forms an ideal shape.

**Diagram 15**

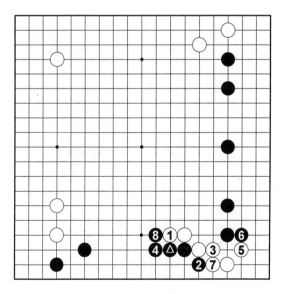

**Diagram 16 -
White's Shape Collapses**
After black extends to ▲, if white does not descend to 2 and simply extends to 1, then black's severe hane at 2 leads to the collapse of white's shape. After the exchange of 5 and 6, white is forced to form an over concentrated shape at 7. White suffers.

**Diagram 16**

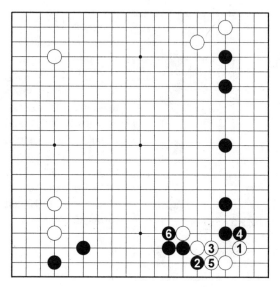

**Diagram 17**

**Diagram 17 -
White Suffers**
White establishes a base with 1. Black 2 is a sente attack which narrows white's base. With the sequence through 6, black forms a broad framework on both sides. Note that 2 is a mutual vital point.

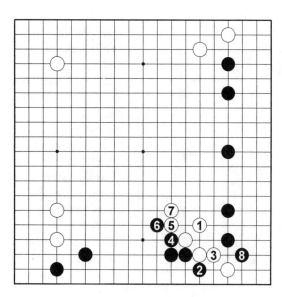

**Diagram 18**

**Diagram 18 -
Black Successfully
Settles Both Groups**
After the tiger at white 1, black attacks with sente at 2. White 3 gives the impression of a clumsy defense. White reinforces at 5 and 7. After black diagonals at 8, black has successfully settled both of his groups.

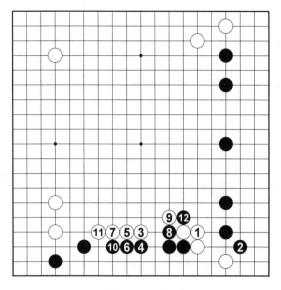

**Diagram 19**

**Diagram 19 -
The Battle Does Not
Favor White**
If white connects at 1
instead, black defends
the corner with a diag-
onal at 2. White gets
outward influence
with the sequence
from 3 to 10. Black's
cut at 12 is severe.
The battle does not
favor white. As a re-
sult, white's connec-
tion at 1 does not
work.

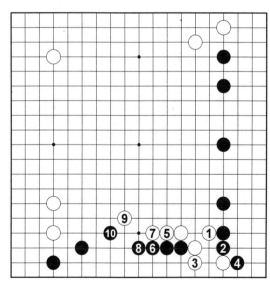

**Diagram 20**

**Diagram 20 -
Black's Territory Is
Big**
White's tiger at 1 is a
power play to settle
his group at the ex-
pense of black's
weakness. White's
descent to 3 in reply to
black's hit at 2 pays
too much attention to
shape. Black's hane
at 4 is a strong attack
gaining territory. Al-
though white builds
up outward influence,
black's territory is
clearly superior.

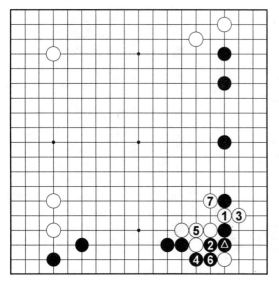

**Diagram 21**

**Diagram 21 -
White Succeeds**

After black hits at ▲, white probes black with the wedge at 1. Black delineates his territory with 2 and 4. On the other hand, white successfully separates the upper and lower black groups by sacrificing a stone in the corner.

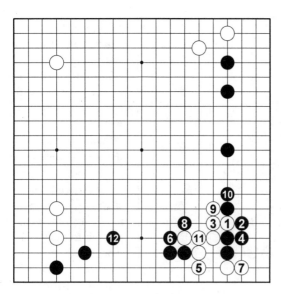

**Diagram 22**

**Diagram 22 -
Black Is Favored**

Black connects at 2 and 4 in reply to the wedge at white 1. If white occupies a vital point for shape at 5, black successfully settles both of his groups with the sequence from 6 to 12. White suffers.

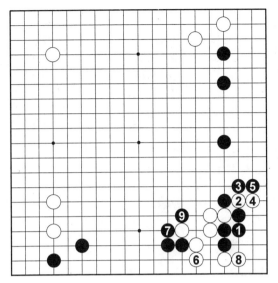

**Diagram 23**

## Diagram 23 -
## Black Is Clearly
## Ahead In Territory

If white cuts at 2 (instead of white 5 in previous diagram) in reply to black's connection at 1, black's calm ataris at 3 and 5 trap two white stones. White then settles his shape by descending to 6. After black seals off white with 7 and 9, black is clearly ahead in territory.

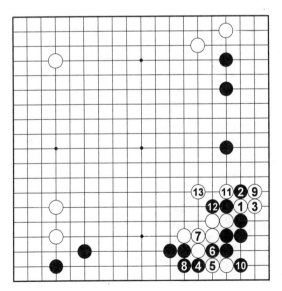

**Diagram 24**

## Diagram 24 -
## Black Suffers Dearly

Black's hane at 4 (instead of descending to 5 in the previous diagram) is an unreasonable reply to white's descent at 3. White 5 is a tesuji. With sente, white double ataris at 11. If black tries to escape with 12, white fences in the two black stones with 13. Black suffers dearly.

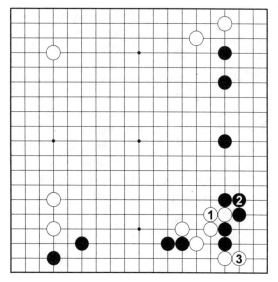

Diagram 25

### Diagram 25 - White Is Satisfied

When white connects at 1 (3 in **Diagram 22**), if black connects at 2, white's crawl along the second line at 3 is big as far as territory is concerned. White builds territory and settles his group at no cost. White can be satisfied.

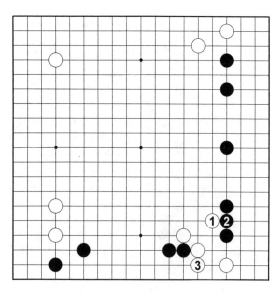

Diagram 26

### Diagram 26 - White's Risk

When white peeps at 1, black is forced to connect at 2 to prevent the cut. This is kind of risky for white. After black connects at 2, white has to descend to 3 to settle his shape. The merit of white 1 and 3 depends on black's responses.

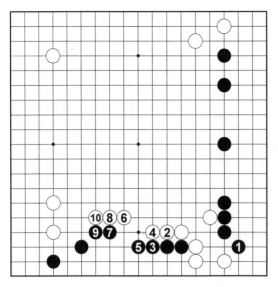

Diagram 27

### Diagram 27 - The Intention Of The Novel Peep

White hopes that black will defend the corner at 1, then white will build up outward influence. Although black builds territory on both sides, white can be satisfied with the outward influence.

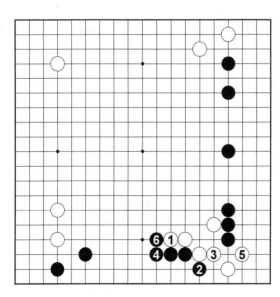

Diagram 28

### Diagram 28 - Difference In Play Order

White extends to 1 (instead of descending to 3 in **Diagram 26**), hoping to descend to 2 after black extends to 4. However, black unexpectedly hanes at 2 spoiling white's plan. Black forms ideal shape with the sequence through 6. On the contrary, white's shape is not good.

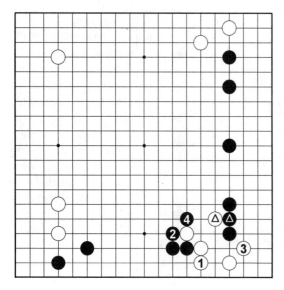

Diagram 29

### Diagram 29 -
### A Blind Spot Of The
### Novel Peep

If black turns at 2 (instead of defending at 3) in reply to white's descent at 1, the novel peep fails. Black's atari at 4 following white's diagonal at 3 seals white in. As a result, the exchange of △ and ▲ is bad for white.

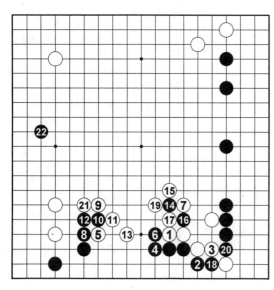

Diagram 30

### Diagram 30 -
### Actual Game

In the actual game, Cho extended to 1, and suffered dearly after black's sente hane at 2. White's shoulder hit at 5 after black's extension to 4, shows Cho's sensitive perception. White creates outward influence through 20. On the other hand, black builds up substantial territory on both sides.

# Chapter Nine
# A Novel Invasion In A Lightning Tournament

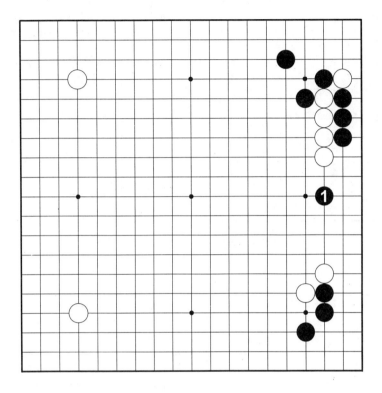

This game is from the quarter final of the 11th Wangwi Tournament. So Pong-su (So Bong-su) took white against Yang Chae-ho (Yang Jaeho). Yang is a member of the Chong-an Baduk Research Institute, together with other renown players like Lee Changho, Yu Chang-hyok (Yoo Chang-hyeok) and Ch'oe Kyu-pyong (Choi Kyu-byung. These players can be considered as the movers and shakers of the Korean Go scene. The novel invasion at 1 was played by Yang in a lightning match. Due to the time limitation, most players are reluctant to try novel plays in a lightning match. However, according to Yang, this novel invasion was invented and analyzed in detail by the Chong-am Baduk Research Institute.

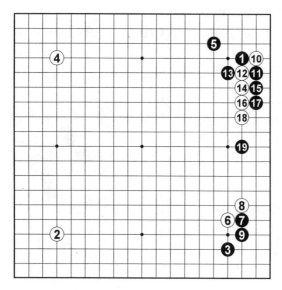

**Diagram 1**

## Diagram 1 - Actual Game

Black 1, 3 and 5 is a solid opening. White counters with a fast-paced 2 and 4. White neglects the development of the joseki on the lower right corner and attaches at 10 instead on the upper right. After 18, black invades at 19, cutting white's connection on the side.

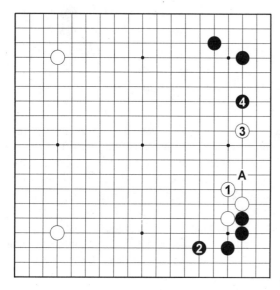

**Diagram 2**

## Diagram 2 - Conventional Approach

White's conventional approach is to tiger at 1 (instead of attaching at 10 in the previous diagram). When black reinforces at 2, white jumps out to 3. Black can split the left side with 4. However, it is more active to attack by jumping to 4 aiming to invade at **A**.

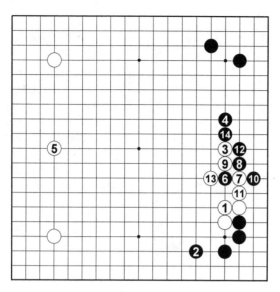

**Diagram 3**

### Diagram 3 - Other Maneuvers

To be consistent with the nirensei (two star opening) strategy, white can also connect at 1. After black's jump to 2, white's jump to 3 is precalculated. Now when black extends and approaches at 4, white can ignore it and complete a sanrensei (three star opening) on the left with 5. The sequence through 13 often appears in actual games.

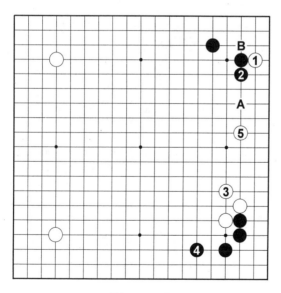

**Diagram 4**

### Diagram 4 - Taken Advantage of by White

Black's extension at 2 forming an over concentrated shape is what white anticipates with 1. A jump to black **A**, following white 3 and 5 is too congested for black. Moreover, with white's attachment at 1, there is a weakness at **B** in the upper right black corner.

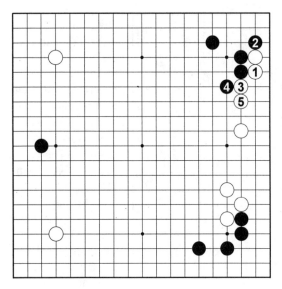

**Diagram 5**

## Diagram 5 - White's Follow-up Maneuver

If black neglects **A** in the previous diagram, then white's extension at 1 is strong. With the sequence from 2 to 5, white secures large territory on the right. If black extends to 3 with 2, then white will hane at 3-3 and get a big corner instead.

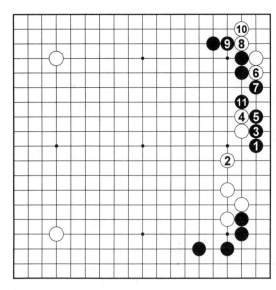

**Diagram 6**

## Diagram 6 - Black's Follow-up Maneuver

Black turning at 6 with 1 is too thick for black. In an international tournament, Cho Chikun invaded at 1 and obtained a favorable position with the sequence from 2 to 11. After the game, analyses from all sources indicated that the result is good for black.

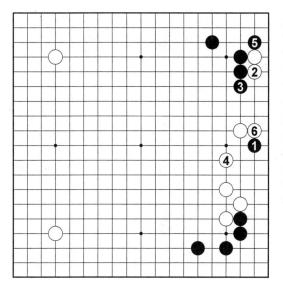

Diagram 7

### Diagram 7 - White's Counter Tactics

White's extension at 2 in reply to black's invasion at 1 is a calculated counter measure to cut black's connection. White cuts off one black stone with the sequence from 3 to 6 and is thick.

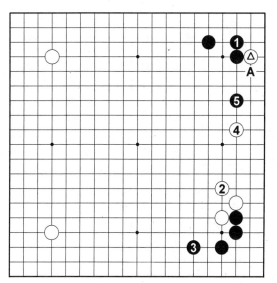

Diagram 8

### Diagram 8 - Black Is Passive

Black's extension at 1 preventing white from making life in the corner at 1 is an overly passive response to the attachment at Δ. After the sequence from 2 to 5, white still has the potential to make life in the corner. The situation favors black if he has a stone at **A**.

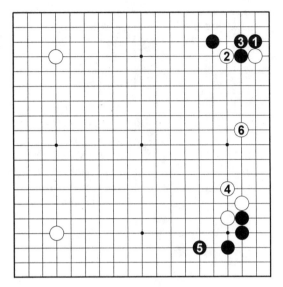

**Diagram 9**

### Diagram 9 - White Taking Advantage

White's clamp at 2 is crucial in reply to black's hane at 1 for defense. White's tiger at 4 and extension at 6 following black's connection at 3 are good rhythm in coordination with 2.

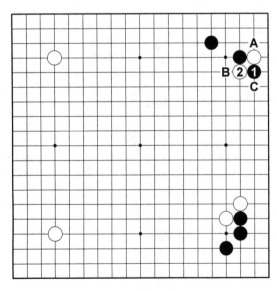

**Diagram 10**

### Diagram 10 - A Powerful Hane

Black's hane at 1 is powerful. White's cut at 2 is a common tactic for seeking more aji. Black can choose to reply at either **A**, **B**, or **C**.

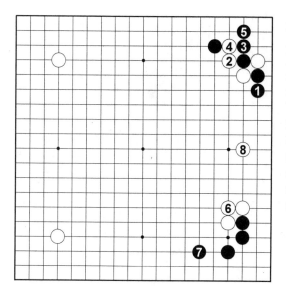

**Diagram 11 -
A Simple Choice**
Black's extension to 1 is a simple yet powerful maneuver. White's sente atari at 2 and poke at 4, followed by the sequence through 8 is commonly seen in professional games. Both sides can be satisfied.

Diagram 11

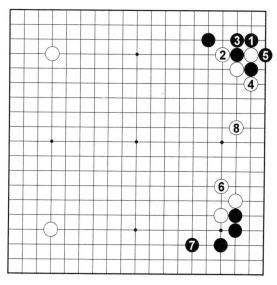

**Diagram 12 -
White Is Flexible**
The atari at 1 reveals black's emphasis on the corner territory. However, white takes advantage with 2 and 4 and can be satisfied with his flexibility.

Diagram 12

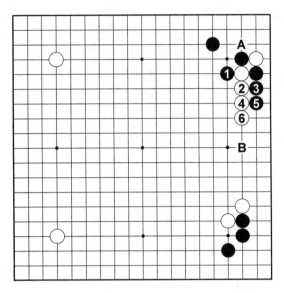

**Diagram 13**

### Diagram 13 - Most Powerful Replies

The atari at 1 and the extension at 3 are the best and most powerful replies. The sequence through 6 is the necessary play order for either side. Black can then choose to descend to **A**, or invade at **B**.

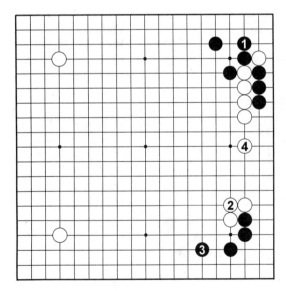

**Diagram 14**

### Diagram 14 - White Is Thick

Black's extension to 1, followed by white 2 and 4 come from a game between Lee Changho and Cho Hunhyun 9 dan. White is considered thick here. On the contrary, black's upper right corner is not well defined.

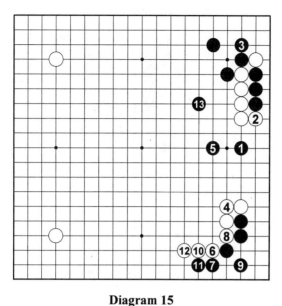

**Diagram 15 - Intention Of The Novel Invasion**
Black's novel invasion at 1 cutting off white's retreat is a strong attack. When white cuts off black's connection at 2, black reinforces at 3. The sequence from 4 to 13 favors black.

**Diagram 15**

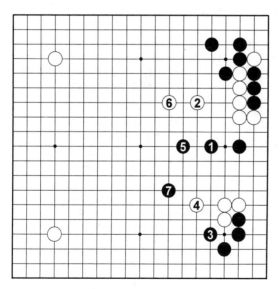

**Diagram 16 - White Is Isolated**
When black jumps to 1, white accordingly jumps out to 2. With black 3 and 5, white is under attack from both sides and this does not favor white. Although white settles his dragon on the top with 6, black attacks white's bottom dragon with 7, and the position favors black.

**Diagram 16**

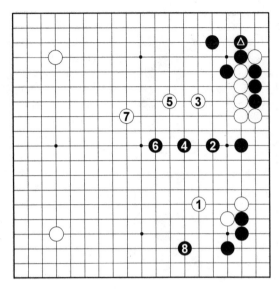

**Diagram 17**

### Diagram 17 - Black Is Slightly Favored

When black reinforces at ▲, white's jump to 1 prevents white from becoming over concentrated. The sequence from 2 to 8 still favors black.

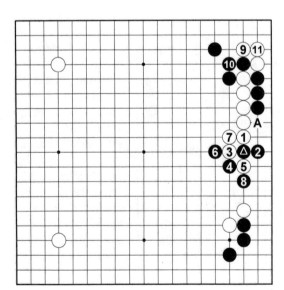

**Diagram 18**

### Diagram 18 - White Succeeds

When black invades at ▲, it's better for white to hit at 1 than turning at **A**. If black descends to 2, white's hane at 3 and cut at 5 are an exquisite maneuver. After securing the corner territory with 9 and 11, white succeeds.

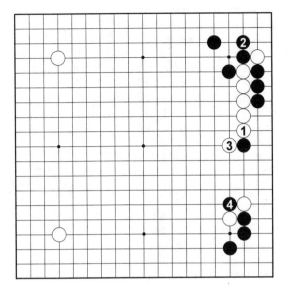

## Diagram 19 - White Is Not Satisfied

Black's defending the corner at 2 in reply to white's hit at 1 is solid. Although white controls a black stone with the hane at 3, the position still slightly favors black after black cuts at 4.

**Diagram 19**

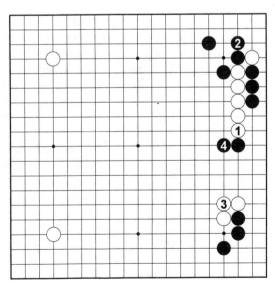

## Diagram 20 - White Suffers

White connecting at 3 instead of a hane at 4 is a big mistake. Black extends to 4 and white suffers.

**Diagram 20**

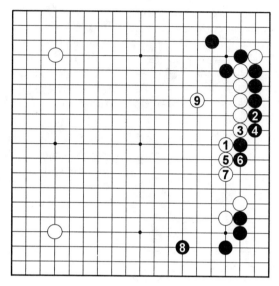

**Diagram 21**

**Diagram 21 -
Black Is Satisfactory**
What if white attaches at 1 instead of hitting at 3? Black connects with 2, 4, and 6, repairing his corner weakness. White's achievement is not big. White tries to settle his group with 7 and 9, but black is satisfactory after extending to 8.

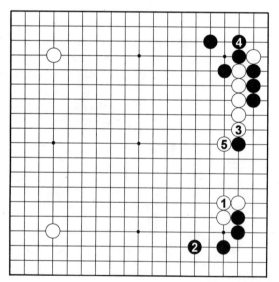

**Diagram 22**

**Diagram 22 -
Correct Play Order**
After the exchange of 1 for 2, white's hit at 3 is correct order. After black reinforces the corner at 4 white then hanes at 5. As a result, black gets territory in both corners and white is thick on the right while controlling a black stone.

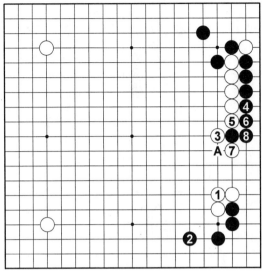

**Diagram 23**

**Diagram 23 -
Black Has The
Upper Hand**
White attaches at 3
instead, hoping black
will reinforce in the
corner, so that white
can control a black
stone as in the previ-
ous diagram. How-
ever, this is a mistake.
Black is not in a hurry
to reinforce the cor-
ner, and connects with
4, 6 and 8 instead.
Due to the presence of
the cutting point at **A**,
the position favors
black.

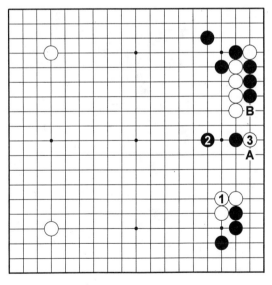

**Diagram 24**

**Diagram 24 -
An Imminent
Counter Attack**
When white connects
at 1, black's jump to 2
is a completely differ-
ent maneuver than in
**Diagram 23**. White
attaches at 3 to probe
black. The outcome
can be entirely differ-
ent depending on
whether black replies
at **A** or **B**.

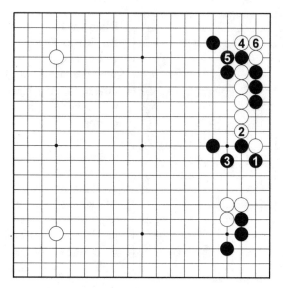

**Diagram 25**

**Diagram 25 - White Succeeds**

Black's hane at 1 is very bad. White hits with sente at 2, before securing territory in the corner with 4 and 6. White succeeds.

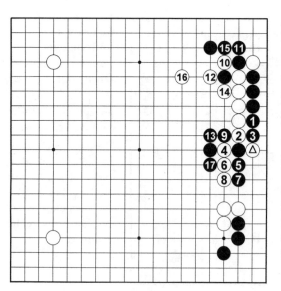

**Diagram 26**

**Diagram 26 - Black Succeeds**

When white attaches at Δ, black can connect with 1 and 3. After white gets outward influence with 4, 6, and 8, black can powerfully cut at 9. White desperately tries to get to the center with the sequence from 10 to 16. However, after extending to 17, black succeeds.

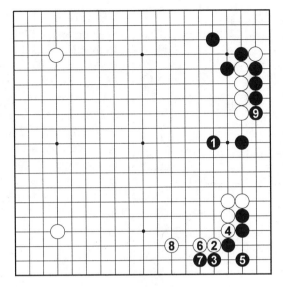

**Diagram 27**

## Diagram 27 - The Result Of The Novel Invasion

When black jumps to 1, a basic maneuver is to attach at 2. A tenuki after the sequence from 3 to 8 is joseki. White develops thickness on the lower right, but black controls the upper right corner by extending to 9. Both sides are satisfied.

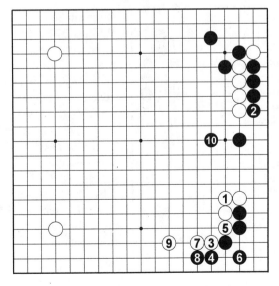

**Diagram 28**

## Diagram 28 - Same Result

When white connects at 1, black can extend to 2 instead. Black then jumps out to 10 after the sequence from 3 to 9, and the result is identical to **Diagram 27**. The only difference is the play order.

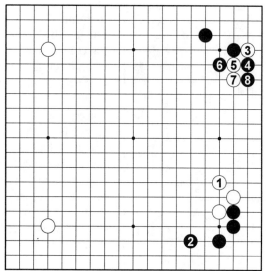

**Diagram 29**

## Diagram 29 - Settling Shape First

Both sides settle their shapes with the exchange of 1 and 2. When white attaches at 3, the result is completely different. The sequence from 4 to 8 is the expected play order. This is white's most powerful response.

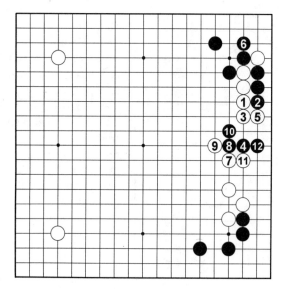

**Diagram 30**

## Diagram 30 - White's Difficulty

Continuing from the previous diagram, black will certainly invade at 4 to cut off white's retreat. White 5, in trying to cut off black's connection is unreasonable. Although white forcefully attacks at 7 and 9, black's turn at 10 puts white in a difficult position.

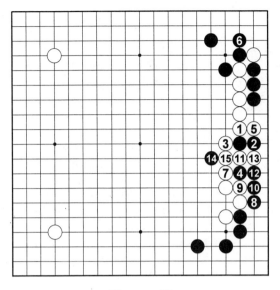

**Diagram 31 - Outward Influence Versus Real Territory**

The hit at 1 cutting off black's connection is strong. Black's descent to 2 is a powerful sacrifice. Black gets real territory on the inside and white counters with thick outward influence

Diagram 31

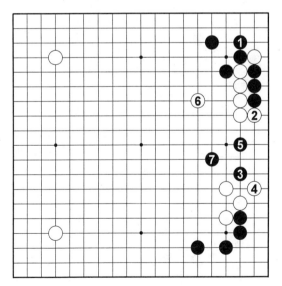

**Diagram 32 - Difficult For White**

A calm reinforcement at 1 in the corner is basic knowledge. White's block at 2 is too greedy. Black invades strongly at 3. After black 7, white is cut apart and faces a tough battle ahead.

Diagram 32

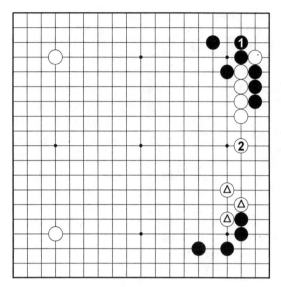

**Diagram 33**

### Diagram 33 - White Is Not Satisfied

White reinforces at 2 instead. But since white 2 is too close to the three Δ stones, white cannot be satisfied. Thus it can be concluded that forming a white tiger on the lower right corner is not appropriate.

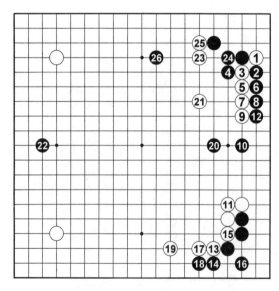

**Diagram 34**

### Diagram 34 - Actual Game

When faced with black's novel invasion of 10, the sequence from 11 to 19 is the best way to handle the situation. White's extension at 25 in reply to black's connection at 24 is too heavy.

Black 26 is an urgent point for attack and black's position is not bad. White won by resignation in 152 plays.

# Chapter Ten
# A Novel Invasion That Claims Victory
# for the Challenger

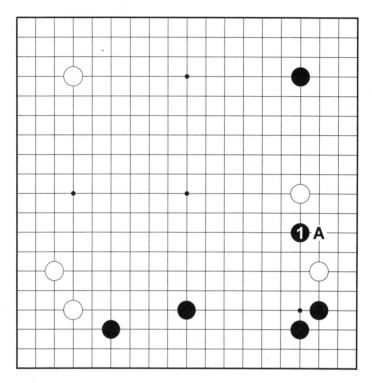

**Example 10**

This game is from the 16$^{th}$ Gukgi Tournament. Yu Chang-hyok (Yoo Chang-hyeok) took white against Lee Chang-ho (Yi Chang-ho) and were playing to determine the challenger for the Gukgi title. Generally speaking, black's invasion at 1, which allows white to connect by attaching at **A**, will be criticized by professional players. After the game, Lee admitted that he never planned on the play but rather made it impulsively during the game. The interesting thing was, Yu seemed to be baffled by this invasion and did not know what to do. He then made one bad play after another and eventually lost the game. Let us analyze this novel invasion which is seemingly against the go theory.

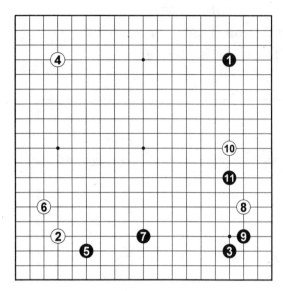

**Diagram 1**

### Diagram 1 - Actual Game

The sequence through 7 is a very common fuseki. When white approaches the lower right corner at 8, black's diagonal at 9 adopts the strategy of getting real territory. Although white's extension at 10 looks uninspired, it stresses speed. Black 11 is the novel invasion.

**Diagram 2**

### Diagram 2 - Conventional Approach

White's extension to 3 in reply to black's reinforcement at 2 is the conventional approach. Black forces at 4. When white jumps to 5, black reinforces the bottom with 6. Both sides can be satisfied.

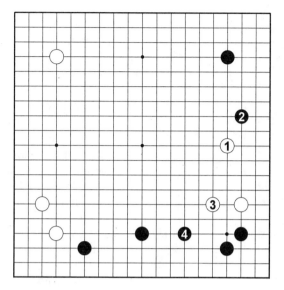

**Diagram 3 -
Another Common
Approach**
When white jumps to
1, a forcing attack at 2
is common sense.
Following the ex-
change of white 3 for
black 4, an extension
by white on the top of
the board is a common
position seen in actual
games.

**Diagram 3**

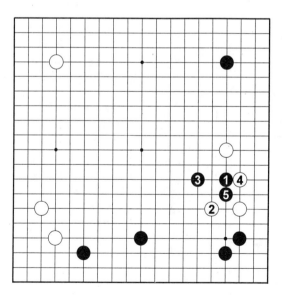

**Diagram 4 -
Unreasonable For
White**
White's jump to 2 is
an unreasonable reply
to black's invasion at
1. After black jumps
to 3, white tries to
connect underneath.
Black 5 aims at
white's weak links
and white fails.

**Diagram 4**

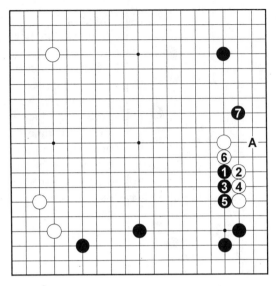

**Diagram 5**

## Diagram 5 - An Excellent Forcing Play

After the exchange of black 1 for white 2, black extends to 3. When black extends to 5, white hits at 6 to settle his shape. Black's forcing attack at 7 is deadly. White has no follow up. Allowing black to occupy **A** will take away white's base. Even if white is able to reinforce at **A**, it's not a desirable position for white.

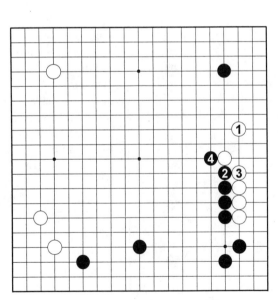

**Diagram 6**

## Diagram 6 - White Is Worse

Since white is not willing to create the result of **Diagram 5**, he jumps to 1 instead. However, black blocks white with 2 and 4 and expands his moyo on the bottom. This result is even better for black than **Diagram 5**.

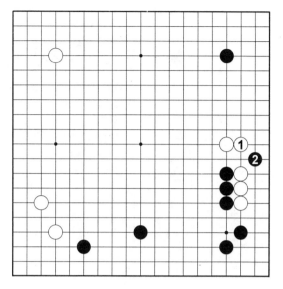

**Diagram 7 -**
**Excellent Timing**
White's extension at 1 allows black to peep at 2 and is very bad for white. Regardless of which side white blocks on, black can utilize sacrifice tactics.

**Diagram 7**

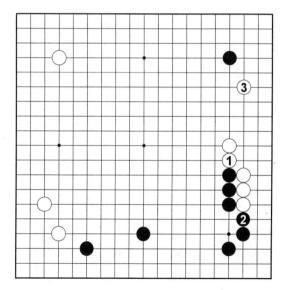

**Diagram 8 -**
**Black Is Falling**
**Behind**
Black's block at 2 in response to white's hit at 1 is too passive. White's approach at 3 is an excellent maneuver. Although black is thick on the lower right corner, black is falling behind due to white's excellent shape with 3.

**Diagram 8**

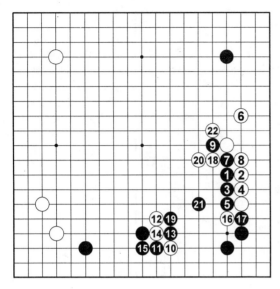

**Diagram 9**

## Diagram 9 -
## Although the Ladder Is Unfavorable Black Is Better off

Black can be considered successful after 9. White's invasion at 10 is premature. Even if the ladder does not favor black, the sequence from 11 to 15 does not favor white. Black won by resignation in 139 plays.

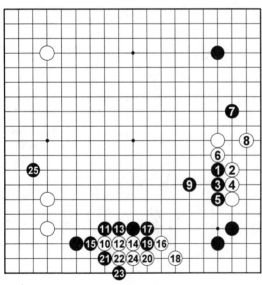

**Diagram 10**

## Diagram 10 -
## Another Example

This example is taken from the second round of the Pae Wang Tournament, with Im Son-kun 8 dan taking black against Kang Chol-min 7 dan. Black's jump to 9 gives black a thick moyo. Black handles white's invasion at 10 keeping sente to 24, before the excellent attack at 25. Black is favored and won by resignation in 229 plays.

# Chapter Eleven
## A Novel Extension
## The Momentum of a Young Player

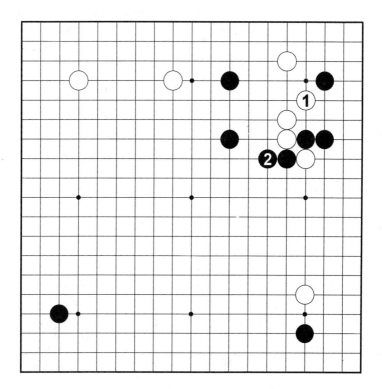

**Example 11**

This is the second game of the 28th Pae Wang Tournament with Cho Hun-hyun taking white against Yun Song-hyon 3 dan. At the time Cho had held the Pae Wang title for 16 consecutive years. Yun on the other hand was known as one of the top four new innovative players. Cho took the first game. In the second game, Cho made an early play order mistake at 1 in the upper right corner, leading to an aggressive novel extension at 2 by the challenger. Skill is naturally important in a tournament, but the impact of psychological factors cannot be overemphasized. Therefore momentum is crucial in a tournament. Let us analyze this novel extension.

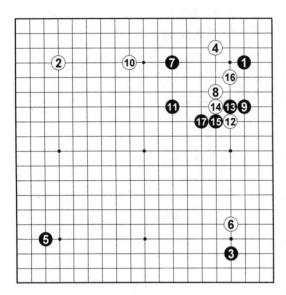

**Diagram 1**

## Diagram 1 - Actual Game

Black 1, 3, and 5 are the famous Shusaku Fuseki. Black's push and cut with 13 and 15 show the aggressive attack of a young player. Cho's diagonal at 16 is a play order mistake. Black gains the momentum with his novel extension at 17.

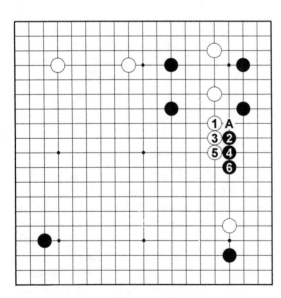

**Diagram 2**

## Diagram 2 - Black Has Big Territory

White's jump to 1 instead of blocking at **A** lacks momentum. Black can be satisfied securing territory on the fourth line with 2, 4 and 6. White can catch up in territory by attacking the two black stones, but has no guarantee for success.

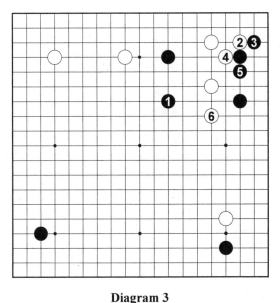

**Diagram 3 -
White Gains The
Advantage**
When black jumps to
1, white can probe at 2
before developing to-
wards the center. Af-
ter black reinforces at
3 and 5, it's important
for white to jump to 6
and not tenuki. White
gets an advantage in
the upper right corner
and is better off.

Diagram 3

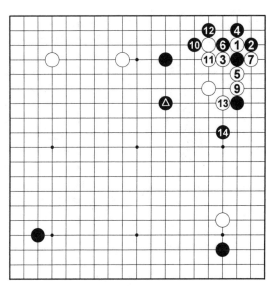

**Diagram 4 -
A Sure Counter
Attack**
Black's atari at 4 in
response to white 3 is
a strong counterattack.
The ataris at white 5
and 7 maintain
white's momentum.
The sequence through
12 is inevitable. After
the exchange of white
13 for black 14, due to
the presence of ▲,
white's outward in-
fluence is contained.
This favors black.

Diagram 4  (8@1)

-171-

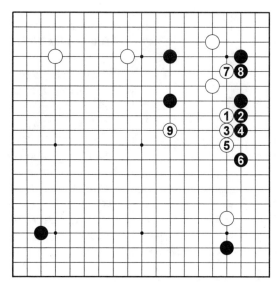

**Diagram 5**

## Diagram 5 - The Conventional Approach

When white blocks at 1, black can simply defend at 2 and 4. The sequence through 8 is a basic joseki, typically leading to a case of outward influence versus real territory. White's cap at 9 is common.

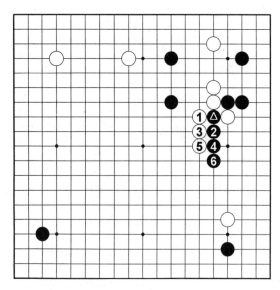

**Diagram 6**

## Diagram 6 - A Typical Slack Atari and Extension

When black cuts at ▲, the atari at white 1 and the extension to 3 are a crude way running towards the center. Black creates a big framework on the right through 6. On the other hand, white has weaknesses in his shape, and this does not favor white.

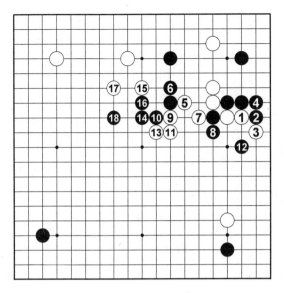

**Diagram 7**

## Diagram 7 - An Exchange

White's block at 1 can be considered. If black hanes at 2, white hanes in sente at 3 and white's attachment at 5 is a tesuji. Black can only extend to 6. White then sacrifices three stones and settles his shape from 7 to 11. Following black 12 through 18, an even exchange results.

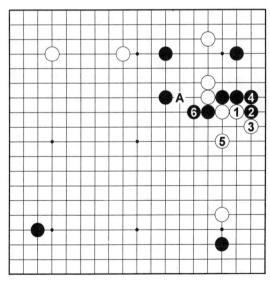

**Diagram 8**

## Diagram 8 - The Battle Favors Black

After black connects at 4, white's jump to 5 instead of attaching at **A** is unreasonable. Black's extension at 6 is strong. White should realize that the battle now favors black.

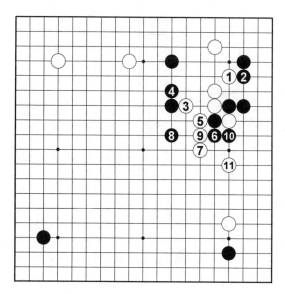

Diagram 9

### Diagram 9 -
### White Is Favored

What happens if white diagonals at 1? Black extends to 2 and white attaches at 3. The play order in the sequence from the drawback to 4 to white 11 is inevitable. This favors white.

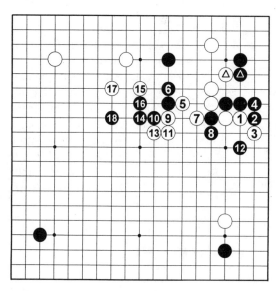

Diagram 10

### Diagram 10 -
### A Mutual Exchange

White can also attach at 5. The sequence from black 6 to 18 results in an exchange that is identical to that in **Diagram 7** except for the presence of △ and ▲. Black's extension to 7 in the next diagram in reply to ▲ is the novel extension.

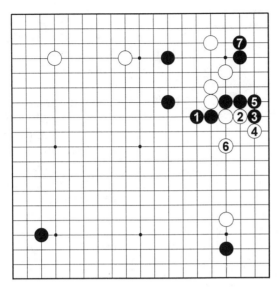

### Diagram 11 - Difficult For White

When black extends to 1, white's all out attack at 2 is unreasonable. The hane at 3 and connection at 5 are the urgent points for good shape. After white jumps to 6, black doubles up at 7. It will be difficult for white to live with his group on the top.

**Diagram 11**

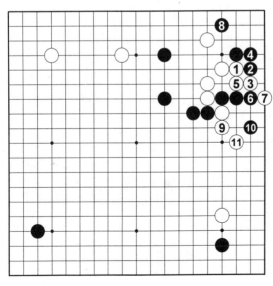

### Diagram 12 - Loss Outweighs Profit

White's thrust at 1 is the best choice. Although black makes life in the corner with 2 to 8, white's extension at 9 makes it difficult for black. When black jumps to 10, white simply diagonals at 11. Black's loss on the side outweighs his gain in the corner.

**Diagram 12**

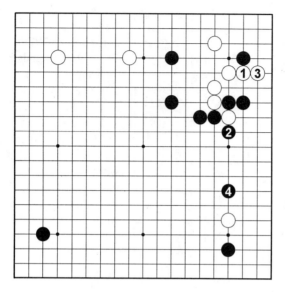

**Diagram 13 -**
**The Conclusion Of**
**The Novel Extension**
Black's atari at 2 in
reply to white's ex-
tension at 1 is the cor-
rect answer. White's
descent to 3 protect-
ing the corner is cru-
cial. As a result, black
gets outward influence
and white gets real
territory. With black's
pincer at 4, black is
ok.

Diagram 13

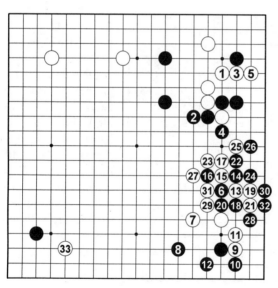

**Diagram 14 -**
**Actual Game**
White gets big terri-
tory with the sequence
from 2 to 5 and is
slightly better off.
White's attachment
and crosscut at 13 and
15 in reply to black's
diagonal at 12 are in-
teresting tactics.
White is successful in
utilizing sacrifice tac-
tics through black 32.
White won by resigna-
tion in 202 plays.

Diagram 14

# Chapter Twelve
## A Powerful Novel Atari

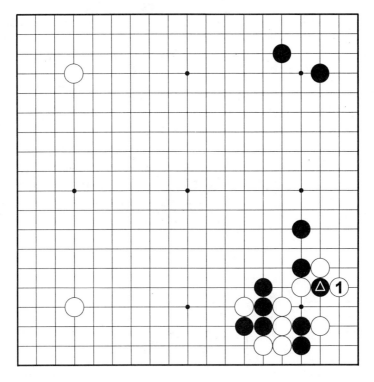

**Example 12**

This example is from a game between two students in Group B of the Korean Baduk Institute. Until 1986, the Korean Baduk Association only allowed its students to participate in the entrance examination of professional players. At that time the only dan level students were Lee Changho 6 dan and Kim Won 5 dan. Of course no one doubted the strength of these professional players who were once students of the institute. How these students would adapt to the professional's life was the question. Black cuts at ▲ trying to utilize sacrifice tactics. White 1 is a powerful novel atari.

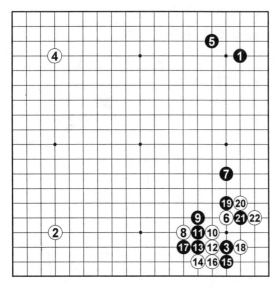

**Diagram 1**

## Diagram 1 - Actual Game

Black's jump to 9 in reply to white's large knight at 8 is an approach which stresses outward influence. Black plans to settle his shape with sente, before taking the big territorial point on the top. The sequence from 10 to 21 forms a common joseki. White 22 is a novel atari.

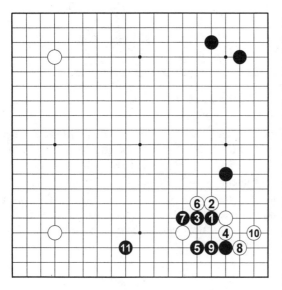

**Diagram 2**

## Diagram 2- Conventional Joseki

In reply to white's large knight's, black's attachment at 1 tries to avoid complicated variations. This is a common joseki. Both sides can be satisfied with the predictable sequence from white's press at 2 to black 11. However, white is more or less dissatisfied with allowing black to easily settle his shape.

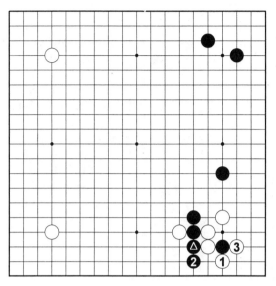

**Diagram 3**

**Diagram 3 -**
**A Simple Reply**
White's hane at 1 is a simple reply to ▲, trying to avoid complicated variations. Black descends to 2 and white captures a black stone with 3. Both sides play with simplicity.

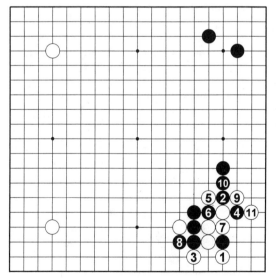

**Diagram 4**

**Diagram 4 -**
**Big Territory**
If black attaches at 2 instead, white hanes at 3. When black hanes at 4, white's hane at 5 is well prepared. Black 6 and 8 are straight forward defenses. After white ataris at 11, white's corner territory is big.

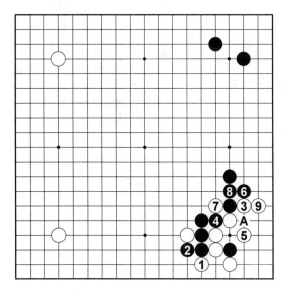

**Diagram 5**

**Diagram 5 -
White Is Better off**

In reply to white's hane at 1, black extends to 2 instead of a hane at **A**. White hanes at 3 and black turns at 4. White tigers at 5 in defense and takes advantage of an opportunity at 7. The development through 9 favors white.

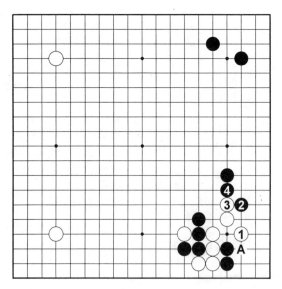

**Diagram 6**

**Diagram 6 -
Black Is Favored**

An attachment at **A** to capture two black stones is a basic defense. White's diagonal at 1 also looks like a strong defense. However, 2 is an urgent point for shape. White is almost sealed off after black 4 and there are still weaknesses in the corner. This does not favor white.

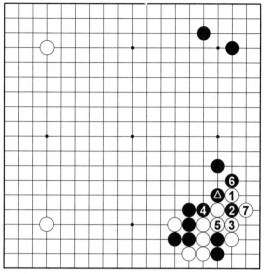

Diagram 7

## Diagram 7 - Basic Joseki

Following ▲, white's hane at 1 and black's cut at 2 are predetermined order. The sequence from white's atari at 3 to 7, forms a basic joseki with black's outward influence countering white's real territory. In comparison with **Diagram 5**, black is able to block with sente on the bottom.

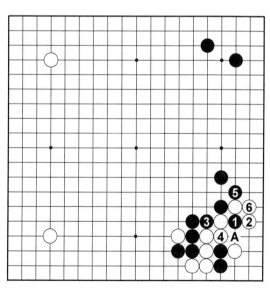

Diagram 8

## Diagram 8 - Intention Of The Novel Atari

White's atari at 2 on the second line instead of at **A** is novel. When white descends to 6, the location of white 2 is more valuable than **A**. Compared to the previous diagram, white has more territory in the corner. Moreover, white can extend into black's territory on the right hand side.

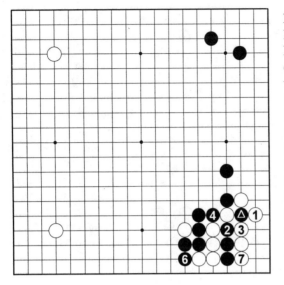

Diagram 9  (5@▲)

### Diagram 9 -
### Black Is Thick

Black 2 is a diametrically opposed reply to white's novel atari at 1. If white captures at 3, black counter-ataris at 4, forcing white to form an over concentrated shape by connecting at 5. Black then forms a thick position by blocking at 6.

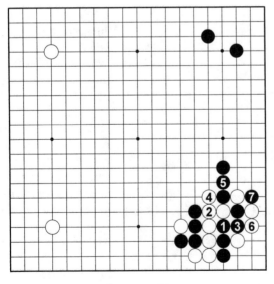

Diagram 10

### Diagram 10 -
### White Is Killed

When black ataris at 1, white's connection at 2 is crucial. Black's connection at 3 is also necessary. However, white's atari at 4 is bad. After black connects at 5, white is forced to connect at 6. After black cuts at 7, white is doomed.

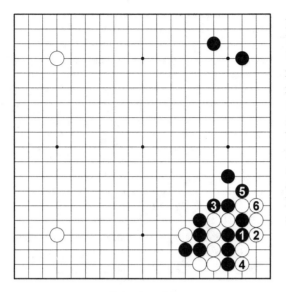

**Diagram 11** **Diagram 11 -**
**White Is Favored**
White's simple connection at 2 is the correct response to black 1. If black blocks at 3, white ataris five black stones at 4 and is better off. This result is similar to that of **Diagram 8** with black's back doors still wide open.

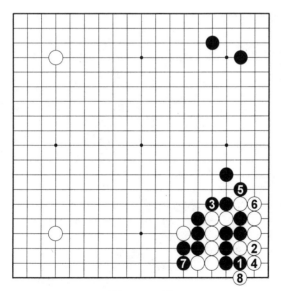

**Diagram 12** **Diagram 1 2 -**
**Black's Over-**
**Whelming Outward**
**Influence**
Black can also atari at 1 first, and block at 3 after white connects at 2. After white reduces the liberties of the six black stones at 4, black seals off white with sente at 7. As a result, black builds up an overwhelming outward influence with only one open back door.

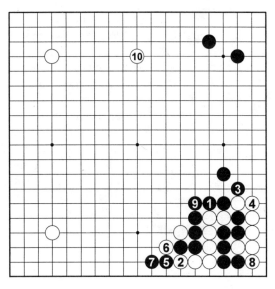

**Diagram 13**

## Diagram 13 - White's Variation

Instead of reducing black's liberties at 8, white answers black 1 with a probe at 2. When black blocks at 5, white's cut at 6 is the key. White takes the big territorial point at 10. Moreover, the two white stones which were cut off, still have potential. White's fast-paced strategy for taking the big territorial point worked.

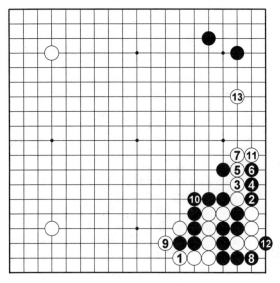

**Diagram 14**

## Diagram 14 - White Is Slightly Favored

If black cuts at 2 in reply to white 1, black gets sente. After the sequence from 3 to 6, black kills four vital white stones. White hanes at 9 and black connects at 10. Locally the sequence through 13 is the best development for both sides. As far as the whole board is concerned, it slightly favors white.

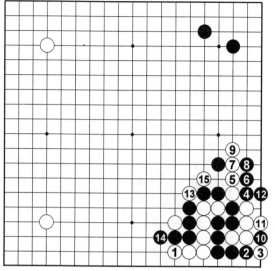

## Diagram 15 - The Ladder

Black occupies the corner with 2 to 12. If the ladder favors white, a hane at 13 is more powerful than a hane at 14. After black extends to 14, white gets a ladder at 15, and black fails. If the ladder favors white, then black's cut at 4 in reply to white 1 does not work.

**Diagram 15**

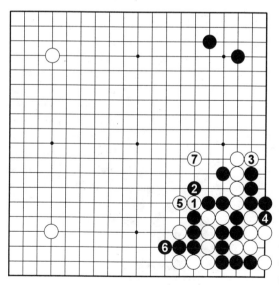

## Diagram 16 - Resistance from Black

In response to white's cut at 1, black tries to avoid a ladder with an atari at 2 with sente. White turns at 3 and extends to 5 in correct order. As a result, black's resistance was useless. Although black stubbornly resists in the corner, white occupies the vital point at 7, putting black in a difficult position.

**Diagram 16**

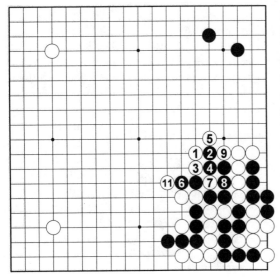

Diagram 17 (10@7)

### Diagram 17 - Black Is Killed

When white occupies the vital point at 1, black's diagonal attachment at 2 is the strongest resistance. White's strong clamp at 3 kills black. Black stubbornly resists with 4 and 6. However, white 11 captures black with a ladder

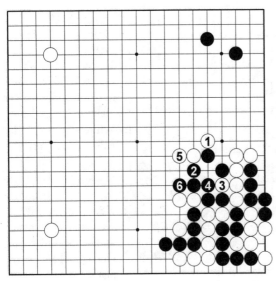

Diagram 18

### Diagram 18 - A Reversion

A white hane at 1 instead of a clamp at the point of black 2 does not work. Black 2 is a mutual vital point. White tries to reduce black's liberties with 3 and 5. However, when black extends to 6, white has no follow up.

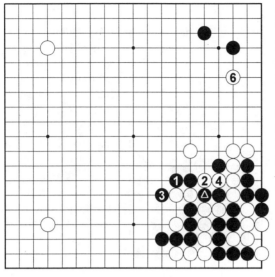

Diagram 19    (5@▲)

### Diagram 19 - White Is Better off

If the ladder is not favorable, it's better for black to extend to 1 instead. White connects his stones with 2 and 4 in sente and follows with an expansion jump to 6 to develop the right side. This absolutely favors white.

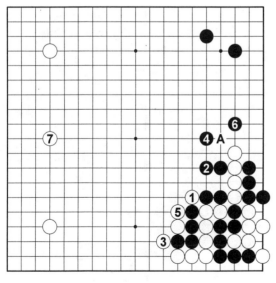

Diagram 20

### Diagram 20 - The Power of Thickness

White 1 followed by black's extension at 2 and white's atari at 3 favors white. When black attacks white on the right with 4 and 6, white 7 fully develops his moyo on the left and white is definitely better off. White's four surrounded stones on the right still have some potential with a white diagonal attachment at **A**.

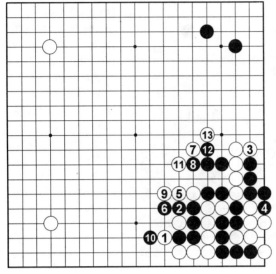

**Diagram 21**

### Diagram 21 - Unreasonable Extension

Black's extension to 2 in reply to white's atari at 1 is unreasonable. After white's sente at 3 and 5, white seals black off at 7 in correct order. When black resists at 8, white's extension at 9 is a precalculated tesuji. Black fails after white 13.

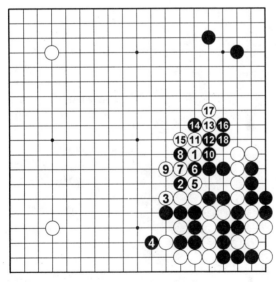

**Diagram 22**

### Diagram 22- White Is Killed

When white blocks at 1, black attaches at 2 trying to confuse white. If white simply attacks with 3, 5, and 7, he falls into black's trap. Black succeeds in killing white with the sequence from 8 to 17.

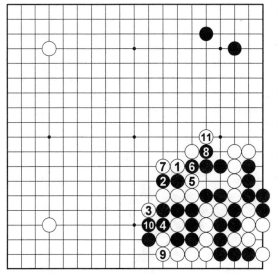

**Diagram 23**

**Diagram 23 -
A Calm Tesuji**
White's attachment at 1 is a calm tesuji. When black escapes at 2, white ataris at 3 and cuts at 5. Even though black resists at 6, white still kills black after 11.

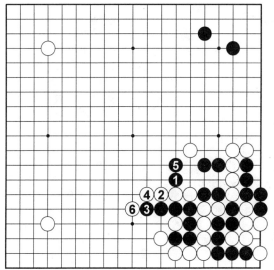

**Diagram 24**

**Diagram 24 -
Black Suffers**
If black extends at 3 in reply to white 2, white's extension at 4 will put black in a difficult position. Black tries to settle his dragon at 5. But after white hanes at 6, the black dragon is again in danger.

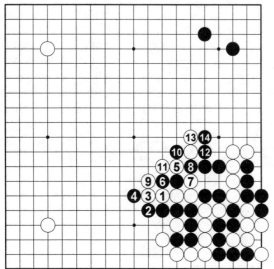

**Diagram 25**

## Diagram 25 -
## White Is Captured

What will happen if black hanes at 4 following white's extensions at 1 and 3? White's clamp at 5 is also a tesuji. White's thrust to 7 is impulsive. White's group on the right is captured with the sequence from 8 to 14.

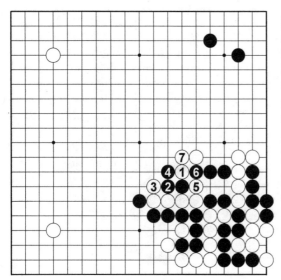

**Diagram 26**

## Diagram 26 -
## A Calm Strong Extension

Following white's clamp at 1 and black's extension at 2, white's extension at 3, instead of first cutting at 5, is calm and strong. White's cut at 5 after black escapes to 4 is correct order. When black ataris at 6, white connects at 7. Black has no follow up.

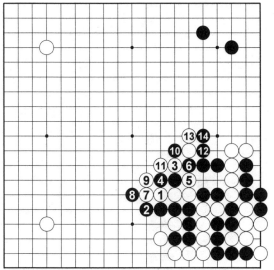

**Diagram 27 - A Hasty Clamp**
White's premature clamp at 3, instead of extending to 7 is a mistake. Black's extension to 4 is powerful. White loses after black 14, because of the hasty clamp.

Diagram 27

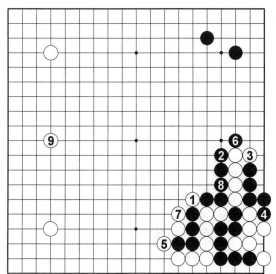

**Diagram 28 - The Result of the Novel Atari**
Since the ladder is favorable, white's cut at 1 is powerful. White will come out ahead, regardless of black's reply. Black's extension at 2 is about the best choice. White captures at 7 with sente before taking the big territorial point at 9. White is absolutely favored here.

Diagram 28

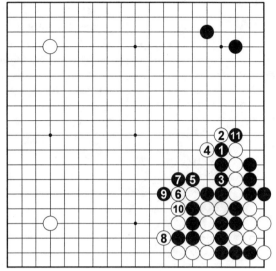

**Diagram 29**

### Diagram 29 - White Is Unreasonable

In reply to black 1, white hanes at 2, trying to attend to both groups. But this is actually unreasonable. Black's connection at 3 is best for attacking white. The sequence through 11 proves that white was unreasonable.

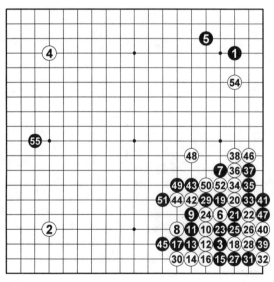

**Diagram 30   (53@29)**

### Diagram 30 - Actual Game

White makes the novel atari at 22 and cuts at 42 because of the favorable ladder. The sequence through white 54 is the best order and best responses from both sides. White is slightly favored from a global point of view.

# Chapter 13
## A Novel Invasion
## The Starting Point of a Lost Game

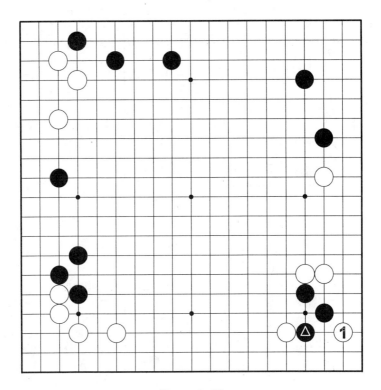

**Example 13**

This example is from the fourth game of a five game tournament in the 32$^{nd}$ Chaigowi (Highest Ranking Tournament). Lee had white against Cho Hun-Hyun. The Chaigowi means a lot to either player, because it was the tournament where both players captured their first title. Entering this game, Lee was behind in the tournament 1 to 2 and thus in a disadvantageous position. White 1 is a novel invasion adopted by Lee in reply to Cho's diagonal attachment at ▲. Because of this novel invasion, Lee lost the game and also his Chaigowi title. Now, let us analyze this novel invasion.

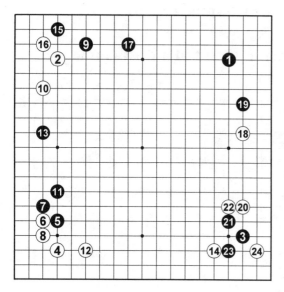

**Diagram 1**

## Diagram 1 - Actual Game

Black 1 to 19 is the actual sequence which took place in the game. White's pincer attack at 20 maintains connection with white 18. Black tries to settle his shape quickly with 21 and 23. White's attack at 24 is the novel invasion.

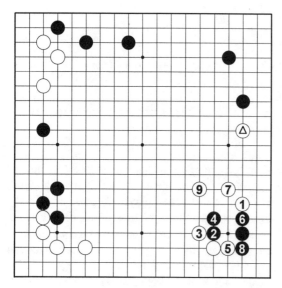

**Diagram 2**

## Diagram 2 - White's Intention

White 1 is a pincer in correlation with Δ. After black settles his group from 2 to 8, white jumps out to 9 to expand his territory on the right. The spacing between white's thickness and Δ is perfect. White's position is very flexible here.

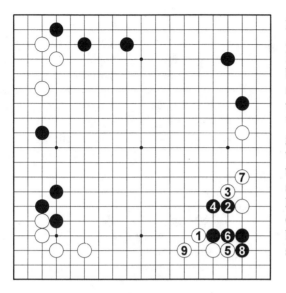

**Diagram 3**

**Diagram 3 -
A Common Sequence**
In response to white 1, black's press at 2 is a strong attachment which probes white. White settles his groups on both sides with the sequence through 9, and can be satisfied. On the other hand, black gets to extend at 8, and can be satisfied with his shape also.

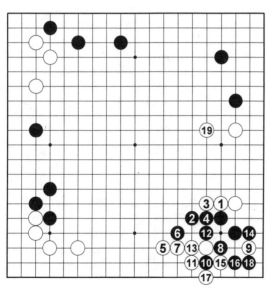

**Diagram 4**

**Diagram 4 -
White Flows
Smoothly**
When white extends to 1, black's jump at 2 instead of a diagonal attachment at 8 is also very common. Black's intention with 2 is to get to the center. The sequence through 18 is a basic joseki in which white obtains sente. White jumps out to 19 and cultivates his territory on the right. This way, white's sequence flows smoothly.

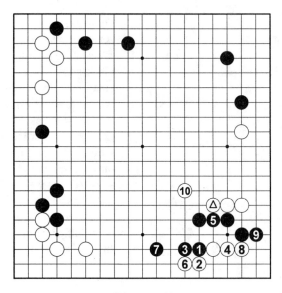

Diagram 5

### Diagram 5 - Black's Profit Is Small

If black 4 in **Diagram 4** attaches at 1, the sequence from 2 to 10 divides white into two groups. Black's profit is small this way, however.

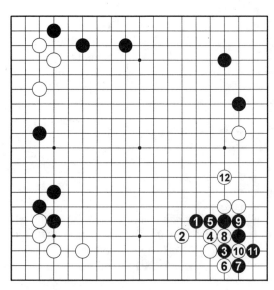

Diagram 6

### Diagram 6 - An Unpredictable Outcome

When black jumps to 1, white can also jump to 2. After black hits at 3, white should be careful. The 4 to 10 sequence leaves aji in the corner. After white reinforces at 12, the corner battle is over. Because of the timing of the ko and the presence of potential ko threats, the outcome of this exchange is difficult to predict.

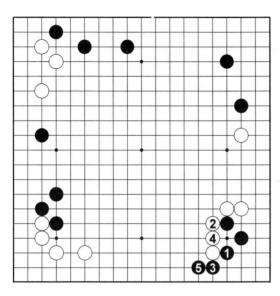

**Diagram 7-**
**Black's Intention**
Black's intention with the diagonal attach-ment at 1 is to settle his shape with 3 and 5, and allow white to reinforce at 2 and 4. The resulting position is very solid for black. On the other hand, white still needs to reinforce his shape before getting enough eye space.

Diagram 7

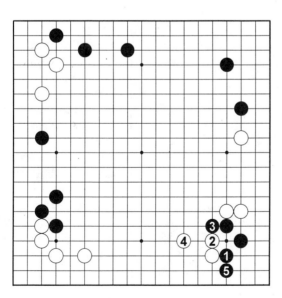

**Diagram 8 -**
**Black Is Successful**
If white extends to 2 in reply to 1, black extends to 3 and white jumps to 4. Black 5 protects his tiger's diagonal links and secures territory at the same time. Black is successful. On the contrary, white seems to be under attack.

Diagram 8

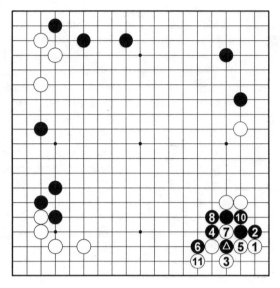

**Diagram 9 (9@▲)**

## Diagram 9 - The Intention Of The Novel Invasion

White's shape attack at 1 is the novel invasion. Its intention is to secure territory with white 3 to 11, if black blocks at 2. Due to the lack of ko threats in the game's beginning, the outcome should favor white.

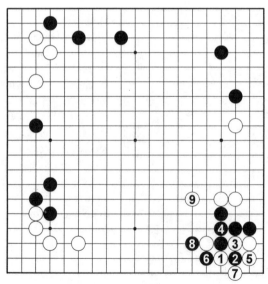

**Diagram 10**

## Diagram 10 - White Successfully Settles His Groups On Both Sides

If black 4 in the previous diagram hanes at 2, white captures a stone with 3 and 5. When black tries to capture a white stone with 6 and 8, white jumps out to 9. White is better off having successfully settled his groups on both sides.

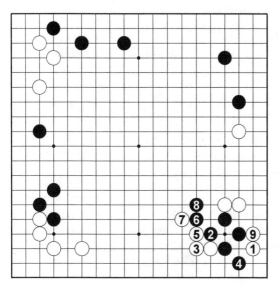

**Diagram 11**

### Diagram 11 -
### Black Floats Without A Base

If black hanes at 2 in reply to the invasion at 1, then white's extension at 3 is firm. Black blocks white from connecting with 4. However, white obtains sente with 5 and 7, before connecting to the other side with 9. The black stones are floating without a base.

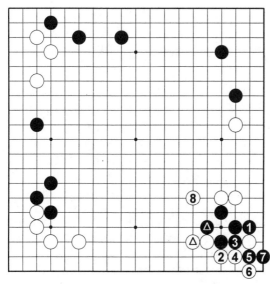

**Diagram 12**

### Diagram 12 -
### Black Is Not Settled

If black 4 in the previous diagram blocks at 1, black captures one stone with 3 and 5. However, white gains an advantage with 4 and 6 before jumping to 8. The black dragon is not settled yet. In considering this novel invasion white envisioned that the exchange of ▲ and Δ will turn black's ▲ into a bad hane.

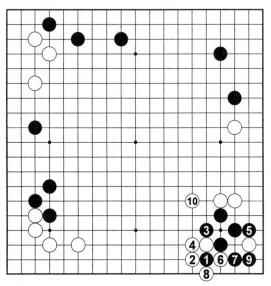

**Diagram 13**

### Diagram 13 - White Has The Upper Hand

Black's hane at 1 is a basic defense. When white counter-hanes at 2, black reaps profit with 3 and 5. Actually, black's loss here outweighs his gain. Although black gets some territory with the sequence through 9, white jumps to 10 and is in a far superior position. Black is not satisfied.

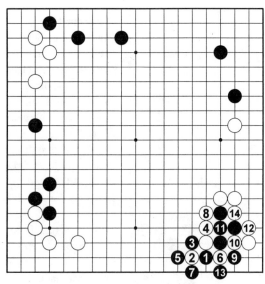

**Diagram 14   (15@6)**

### Diagram 14 - Black Is Slightly Better

If black ataris from the other side and captures a stone with 5 and 7, white ataris at 6 and blocks at 8. The sequence from 9 to 15 represents the best outcome for either side in this situation. Although it looks like white's sacrifice tactics are successful, this is not the case, as black is slightly better off.

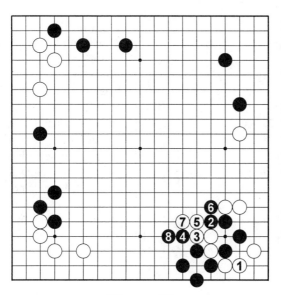

Diagram 15

### Diagram 15 - Difficult For White

It is unreasonable for white to extend to 1 instead of blocking at 2. Black obtains sente with 2 and 4, before turning at 6 to attack white. After white extends at 7, black calmly draws back at 8. This outcome is difficult for white.

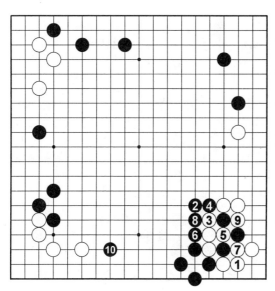

Diagram 16

### Diagram 16 - An Exquisite Tesuji

When white extends to 1, black 2 is an exquisite tesuji, forcing white to extend at 3 and atari at 5. With the sequence to 8, black creates a thick wall with sente. Black then uses the outward influence by extending to 10, and is successful.

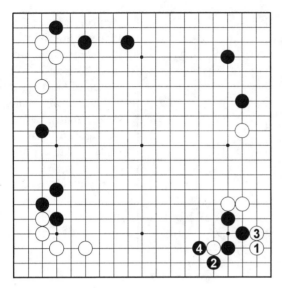

**Diagram 17**

### Diagram 17 - The Result Of A Sente

When white attacks black's corner at 1, black's hane at 2, white's connection at 3, and black's atari at 4 are the best replies to white's novel invasion at 1. Black's position is strengthened after capturing a white stone.

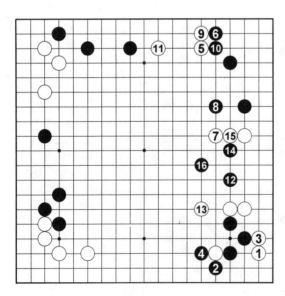

**Diagram 18**

### Diagram 18 - Actual Game

As mentioned above, the sequence from 1 to 4 is the best outcome for either side. After white 5 to 11, black invades at 12. The sequence through 16 favors black. As a result, black won by resignation after 105 plays.

# Chapter 14
## A Novel Clamp in the
## Korean-Japanese New Players Tournament

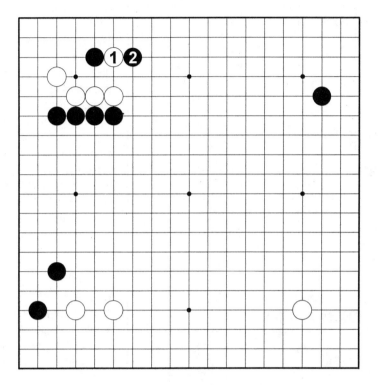

**Example 14**

This example is from the first round of the Korean-Japanese New Players Tournament. Otani of Japan took white against Kim Sung-chun of Korea. Although this tournament, which took place in September of 1993, was unofficial, the participants in this game could be considered as representing the best of the new innovative players in both Japan and Korea. Both countries agreed that this tournament was a test of future Japan and Korea Go strength. In using a novel clamp, Kim was able to take the initiative in the game which ended prematurely in merely 165 plays. With this game, the Korean team beat the Japanese 11 to 9. Let us concentrate on analyzing this interesting novel clamp.

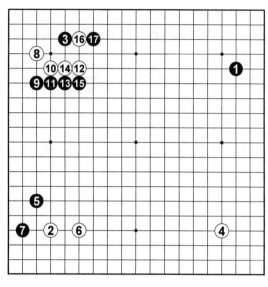

**Diagram 1**

### Diagram 1 - Game

White counters black's consecutive 3-5 fuseki with two consecutive star points opening. The 3-5 fuseki is Kim's favorite opening. When white approaches the corner at 8, black pincers at 9. The sequence through 15 is correct order. In reply to white's attachment at 16, black 17 is a novel clamp.

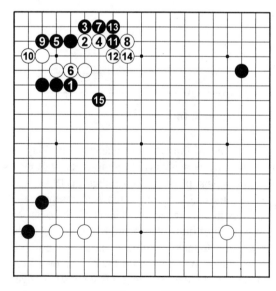

**Diagram 2**

### Diagram 2 - Black Is Better Off

White's attachment at 2 is an effective tactic for handling the potential cut imposed by black's peep at 1. Black settles his shape in sente with 3 to 13, before taking the mutual vital point for attack and defense at 15. This result favors black. White's shape is far from perfect since it's vulnerable to a black attack.

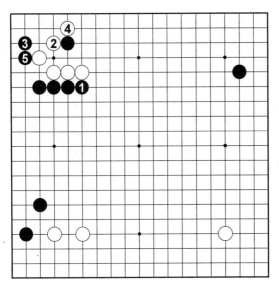

Diagram 3

## Diagram 3 - Black Is Slightly Favored

Following black's extension to 1 and white's tiger at 2, black's attack at 3 is excellent timing. When white hanes at 4, black connects at 5, reaping up real territory. Black is slightly favored.

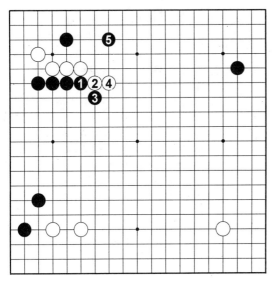

Diagram 4

## Diagram 4 - Black Is Fast-paced

If white hanes at 2 in reply to black 1, black hanes at 3 with sente, before strongly jumping two-spaces to 5. As a result, black successfully settles his two groups. On the other hand, white's shape is heavy and white will face difficult maneuvers ahead.

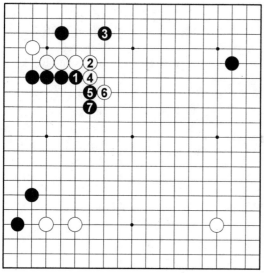

**Diagram 5**

**Diagram 5 -**
**White Is Slack**
White's extension to 2 in reply to black 1 is too slack. When black jumps to 3, white has fallen behind. Although white 4 and 6 solidify white's shape, black naturally strengthens his group with 5 and 7. This does not favor white.

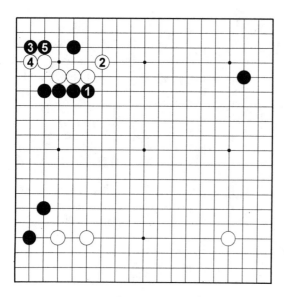

**Diagram 6**

**Diagram 6 -**
**Perfect Timing**
If white diagonals at 2, black attacks at 3 with perfect timing. When white blocks at 4, black secures real territory at 5. If white 4 and black 5 are reversed, it still favors black.

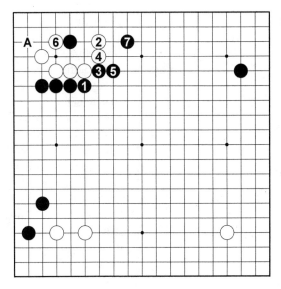

Diagram 7

## Diagram 7 - Weakness

If white jumps to 2, black strongly solidifies his shape with 3 and 5. White defends the weakness at **A** with a tiger at 6 trapping one black stone. However, black confines white with 7 and the result does not favor white.

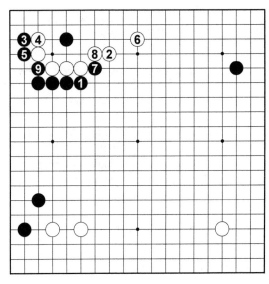

Diagram 8

## Diagram 8 - It's Difficult For White

White jumps to 2 trying to secure territory in the corner. Black attacks white's weakness in the corner at 3. After the 4 - 5 exchange white tries again to gain territory with 6. Unfortunately, white's formation collapses after black 7 and 9.

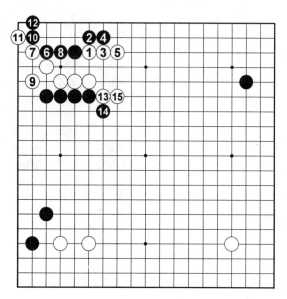

**Diagram 9 -**
**The Conventional**
**Development**

Due to the previous discussions, white's attachment at 1 is the only tactic. Black hanes and extends in sente at 2 and 4, before attaching at 6 to secure his group. This is the conventional approach. The sequence from 7 to 15 is a joseki. Both sides can be satisfied.

**Diagram 9**

**Diagram 10 -**
**White Miscalculated**

If white extends to 1 instead, black takes advantage with the maneuver from 2 to 8. White miscalculated. White settles his shape with 9 and 11. After black reinforces at 12, the result favors black.

**Diagram 10**

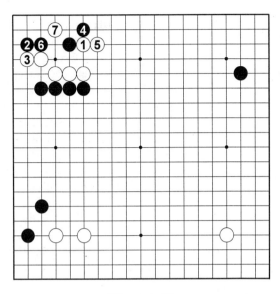

Diagram 11

## Diagram 11 - Black Dies

Black's attack at 2 in reply to white's attachment at 1 is premature. White's block at 3 is strong. Black desperately tries to make life with 4 and 6, but falls short after white's raiding peep at 7.

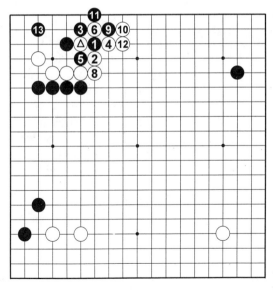

Diagram 12  (7@Δ)

## Diagram 12 - The Intention of the Novel Clamp

Black's attachment at 1 in reply to white's attachment at Δ is a novel clamp. When white hanes at 2, black ataris at 3 and seizes real territory through 13. White's outward influence is clearly inferior to black's territory. Black's novel clamp is successful.

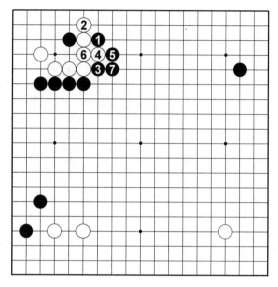

**Diagram 13**

**Diagram 13 -**
**The Result Of The**
**Novel Clamp**
White's descent to 2
in reply to black's at-
tachment at 1 is
strong. Black con-
fines white with 3 and
makes the best con-
nection at 7. Al-
though white's corner
is big, black has over-
whelming outward
influence and both
sides can be satisfied.

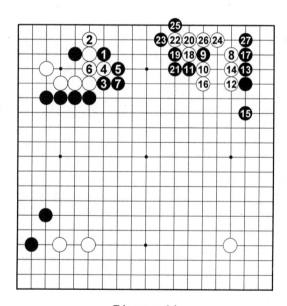

**Diagram 14**

**Diagram 14 -**
**Actual Game**
After black's novel
clamp at 1, the se-
quence from 2 to 6 is
the best choice for
both sides. When
white approaches the
upper right corner at
8, black's pincer at 9
is the only choice of
joseki. Black won by
resignation in 165
plays.

# Chapter 15
# A Novel Hane With Style

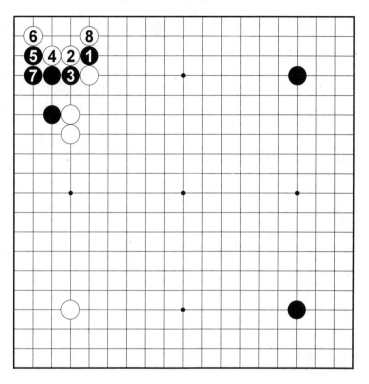

**Example 15**

This example is from the 5th game of the 27th Wangwi Tournament, with Yu Chang-hyok taking white against Cho Hun-hyun. Professional games are often influenced by the player's style. Yu is famous for his attacking style and Cho for his fast-paced rhythm style. In this example, when black attaches at 1, Yu hanes at 2 with a masterpiece of deep consideration. Most professionals liked black's fast-paced and simple approach. Only Yu considered white's slow pace and solid approach as fully acceptable. Let's analyze the variations of this unique novel hane.

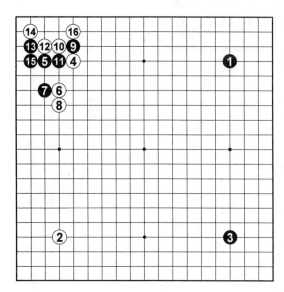

**Diagram 1**

Diagram 1 -
**Actual Game**
White takes the 4-5 point and black enters the corner at 5. When black attaches at 7, white realizes that the ladder is not favorable and adopts tactics for thickness. After black attaches at 9, white hanes at 10. The sequence through white 16 shows the continuation after the novel hane.

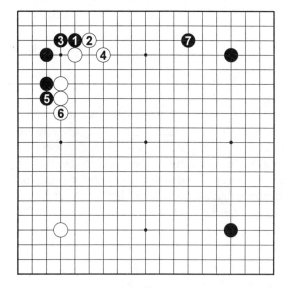

**Diagram 2**

Diagram 2 -
**Conventional Development**
White usually hanes on the outside at 2 in reply to black's attachment at 1. The sequence from 3 to 6 is a basic joseki. Both sides can be satisfied with black getting territory with sente and white getting outward influence. Black 7 contains white's outward influence.

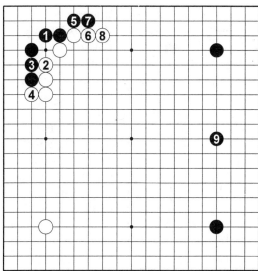

**Diagram 3 - Another Joseki**
When white extends back at 2 and black connects at 3, white solidifies his shape with 4 and 6. Black hanes with sente at 5 and extends at 7 before taking the vital point at 9. Both sides can be satisfied.

**Diagram 3**

**Diagram 4 - Black's Intention**
When black attaches at 1, white cuts with 2 and 4. The connection at 5 is the only defense against white 2 and 4. White 6 is an unreasonable greedy extension to secure territory. Although white manages to make life with the sequence through 10, his confinement far outweighs his gain. After black 11, white is definitely worse off.

**Diagram 4**

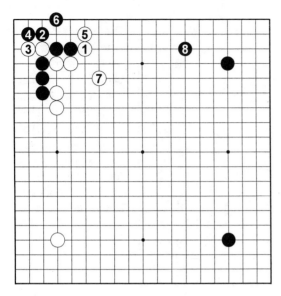

**Diagram 5**

## Diagram 5 - Black Is Slightly Favored

White's hane at 1 is the best choice. When black ataris at 2, white's extension at 3 is crucial. Black gets real territory with the sequence through 7. On the other hand, white gets thickness on the outside. Since black's extension at 8 contains white's influence, the position slightly favors black.

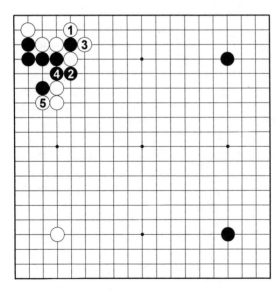

**Diagram 6**

## Diagram 6 - Black Dies

Continuing from **Diagram 1**, when white ataris at 1, black's atari and connection at 2 and 4 are terrible tactics. In breaking through white's enclosure, black allows white to easily capture a stone and when white blocks at 5, black is not settled. This is bad for black.

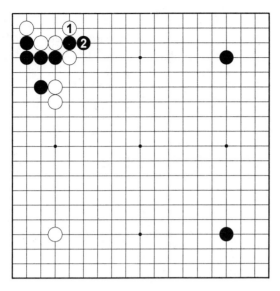

Diagram 7

**Diagram 7 -
The Only Play**
When white ataris at
1, black uncondition-
ally must extend at 2.
Allowing white to
capture a stone is defi-
nitely unfavorable for
black. The develop-
ment is difficult to
predict. Both sides
should be cautious.

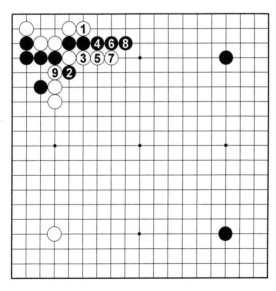

Diagram 8

**Diagram 8 -
Black Is
Unreasonable**
White's extension to 1
is absolutely neces-
sary. However,
black's atari at 2 and
extension at 4 is un-
reasonable. After the
pushing extensions
through 8, white's
sente cut at 9 makes it
difficult for black.

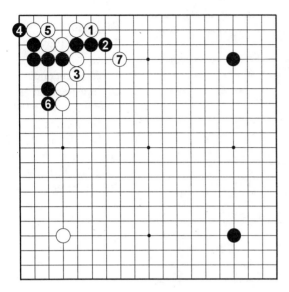

**Diagram 9**

**Diagram 9 -**
**A Horrendous Battle**
White's extension at 1 is a basic defense. White 3 and 5 are correct order. Black's extension at 6 is a mistake. When white extends at 7, black faces a horrendous battle ahead.

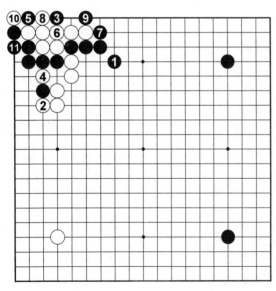

**Diagram 10**

**Diagram 10 -**
**An Approach Ko**
Therefore, black must diagonal at 1 instead of extending to 2. White's block at 2 is unreasonable. Black's peep at 3 is a tesuji for killing white. The sequence from 4 to 11 forms an approach ko.

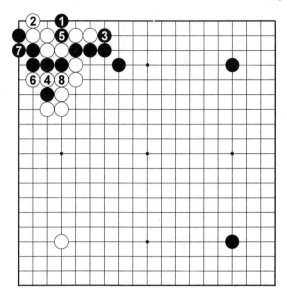

Diagram 11

**Diagram 11 -
Black Falls Into
White's Trap**
White's descent to 2
in reply to black's
peep at 1 tries to cre-
ate an illusion. If
black simply reduces
white's liberties at 3
and 5, he falls into
white's trap and loses
the capturing race by
one play.

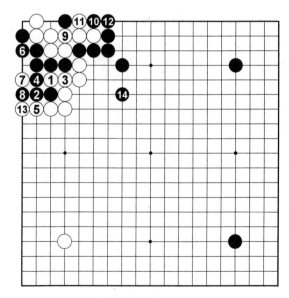

Diagram 12

**Diagram 12 -
Black Is Better Off**
Black 2 in reply to
white 1 is the key to
success. After white
connects at 3, black's
connection at 4 is the
correct order. The
resulting seki with the
sequence from 5 to 13
is the best outcome for
either side. However,
with sente, black
jumps out to 14 to
expand his territorial
framework and white
is worse off.

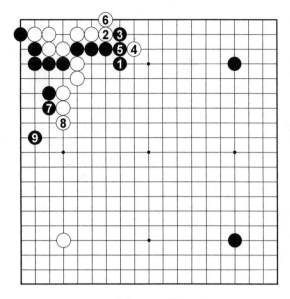

**Diagram 13 -**
**Black Is Favored**
White making life with the sequence from 2 through 6 is the best choice. However, white's extension at 8 in reply to black's push at 7 lacks momentum. Black gains territory by jumping to 9 and is better off.

Diagram 13

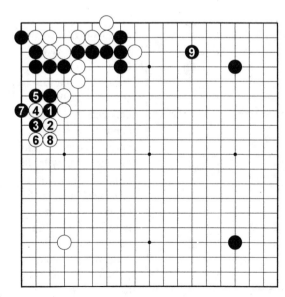

**Diagram 14 -**
**Black Settles Both Of His Groups**
White can consider a hane at 2 in reply to black's extension at 1. The sealing tactics at 4, 6, and 8 are premature. Black takes the big territorial point at 9 and successfully settles both of his groups. white is worse off.

Diagram 14

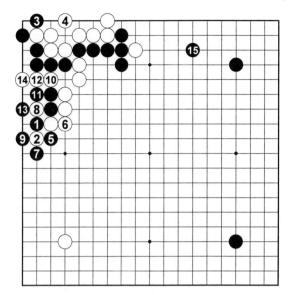

**Diagram 15**

## Diagram 15 - The Result Of The Novel Hane

The two step hane at 2 in reply to black 1 is the basic response. Considering the question of ko threats, black hanes at 3 first. With the sequence through 14, white captures a few black stones. On the other hand, black encloses the upper right corner with a fast pace at 15. Both sides can be satisfied.

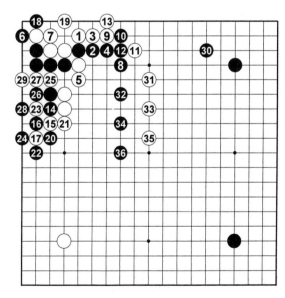

**Diagram 16**

## Diagram 16 - Actual Game

Both sides play in diametrically opposite ways from white 1 to 29. After black encloses the upper right corner with 30, both sides jump out to the center with the sequence through 36. White won by half a point in 260 plays.

# CONCEPTS FOR OUTWARD INFLUENCE

Outward influence consists of broad or narrow thickness or thinness. The power of outward influence is measured by its direction, broadness, narrowness, thickness, and/or thinness.

Outward — not directed towards the edge of the board
Broad — long strings of stones
Narrow — short strings of stones
Thickness — strongly connected strings of stones that cannot be disconnected
Thinness — weakly connected strings of stones that can be disconnected
Power — range of influence

# JAPANESE TERMS FOR GO CONCEPTS

| | |
|---|---|
| aji | The possibilities existing in a position. |
| aji keshi | A play that eliminates possibilities. |
| atari | A play that reduces the liberties of a stone or string of stones to one liberty. |
| chuban | The middle stage of the game. |
| dame | A liberty adjacent to both black and white stones of useless value in Japanese scoring. |
| damezumari | A shortage of liberties. |
| dango | A mass of same color stones clumped together. |
| degiri | A sequence of plays, the first a push between two stones and the second a cut. |
| fuseki | The beginning stage of the game. |
| furikawari | A trade or swap. |
| geta | A tesuji that captures a stone or stones by jumping ahead of them and forming a net. |
| gote | A play with little or no threat value that need not be answered; opposite of sente. |
| guru-guru mawashi | A sequence involving shicho and geta which forces the stones into a dango shape before capturing them. |
| hane | A play that curls around an opponent's stone or string of stones. |
| hamete | A trick play. |
| hasami | A pincer. |
| honte | The proper, more reliable play. |
| horikomi | A sacrifice play that reduces liberties. |
| hoshi | One of the nine marked star points on the go board. |

| | |
|---|---|
| ikken-tobi | A play that is a one point jump. |
| ishi-no-shita | An "under-the-stones" sacrifice. |
| jigo | A game which results in a draw. |
| joseki | A sequence of plays, usually played in the corner, that balances the associated tactical and strategic values of territory, influence, possibilities, and sente. |
| kakari | A play that approaches a single corner stone. |
| kake | A pressing play. |
| karui | Stones with flexible shape. |
| kata | A play that approaches a stone on the diagonal (shoulder hit). |
| katachi | Good shape. |
| keima | Small-knight's shape. |
| kikashi | A forcing play which must be answered. |
| kiri | A play that cuts. |
| ko | A repetitive situation. A play that would create a previous board position, and therefore is not allowed. |
| komi | Compensation points. |
| komoku | A 3-4 point. |
| kori-gatachi | An over concentrated shape. |
| kosumi | A diagonal play. |
| miai | A pair of plays which are virtually equivalent in value such that if one player occupies one of them, the other player will occupy the other. |
| mokuhazushi | A 3-5 point. |
| moyo | A large framework of potential territorial. |
| nakade | An oversized eye shape that can be attacked in such a way that two eyes cannot be made. |
| ni-rensei | A fuseki occupying two corner star points on the same side of the board. |
| nozoki | A play that threatens to cut (peeping play). |
| ogeima | A large-knight's shape. |
| oki | A play which occupies the opponents eye making point. |
| osae | A play that blocks. |
| oshi | A play that pushes. |
| ponnuki | The shape that results from capturing one stone with four stones. |
| ryo-gakari | A play that is a double kakari on the same stone. |
| sabaki | Plays that have many possible threats (much aji). |
| sagari | A play that descends towards the side of the board. |
| san-san | A 3-3 point. |

| | |
|---|---|
| san-rensei | A fuseki occupying three star points on the same side of the board. |
| seki | A position where neither player has two eyes, and neither player can atari the opponent's stones without putting his own stones in atari. |
| semeai | A race between opposing strings of stones attempting to kill each other. |
| sente | A play of such value that should be answered; opposite of gote. |
| shicho | A capture sequence that resembles a ladder. |
| shimari | A two stone corner enclosure. |
| shinogi | A sequence of plays that gives a group of strings good eye making shape. |
| suberi | A play that slides under the opponents stones. |
| suji | A skillful and correct sequence of plays. |
| takamoku | A 4-5 point |
| tenuki | To leave the local situation and play elsewhere. |
| tesuji | A skillful finesse that exploits the possibilities in a position in the most effective manner. |
| tetchu | A play that descends from a stone on a star point that solidifies a side or corner. |
| tewari | A method of analysis in which one changes the order of plays in a sequence and removes superfluous stones in order to evaluate the resulting structure. |
| tobi | A jump play. |
| tsugi | A play that solidly connects. |
| tsuke | A contact or attaching play. |
| tsume | A play that blocks an extension. |
| tsume-Go | A life and death problem. |
| uchikomi | A play that invades. |
| warikomi | A play that wedges in between two enemy stones. |
| yose | The end stage of the game. |

# INDEX

# Other Books From Yutopian

## Sakata Series
Killer of Go
Tesuji and Anti-Suji of Go

## The Nihon Ki-In Series
A Compendium of Trick Plays
100 Challenging Go Problems for 100 Days of Study
Pro-Pro Handicap Go

## Go Handbook Series
Proverbs
Fuseki                                                    (available 2000)

## Chinese Professional Series
Nie WeiPing on Go
Thirty-Six Stratagems Applied to Go, by Ma XiaoChun
Beauty and the Beast, Exquisite Play and Go Theory by Shen Guosun
Golden Opportunities by Rin Kaiho
Winning A Won Game, by Go Seigen
Yang Yilun's Ingenious Life and Death Puzzles, vol. 1 and 2
Essential Joseki by Rui Naiwei
Power Builder, vol. 1, by Wang Runan
Power Builder, vol 2, by Wang Runan          (available 2000)
Strategic Fundamentals in Go, by Guo Tisheng

## Art of Go Series
Art of Connecting Stones
Art of Capturing

## Pocket Book Series, by Yang Yilun
Rescue and Capture
Tricks in Joseki                                         (available 2000)

## Korean Professional Series
Cho HunHyun's Go Techniques, vol. 1
Lee ChangHo's Novel Plays and Shapes

## Other Books From Yutopian
Fighting Ko
Utilizing Outward Influence
Master Go in Ten Days
Dramatic Moments on the Go Board
Igo Hatsuyo-ron, vol. 1